Edgar Walla[illegible] Greenwich and adopted by C[illegible] fish market. At eleven, Walla[illegible] and on leaving school took a [illegible]oyal West Kent Regiment, later transferring to the Medical Staff Corps, and was sent to South Africa. In 1898 he published a collection of poems called *The Mission that Failed*, left the army and became a correspondent for Reuters.

Wallace became the South African war correspondent for *The Daily Mail*. His articles were later published as *Unofficial Dispatches* and his outspokenness infuriated Kitchener, who banned him as a war correspondent until the First World War. He edited the *Rand Daily Mail*, but gambled disastrously on the South African Stock Market, returning to England to report on crimes and hanging trials. He became editor of *The Evening News*, then in 1905 founded the Tallis Press, publishing *Smithy*, a collection of soldier stories, and *Four Just Men*. At various times he worked on *The Standard*, *The Star*, *The Week-End Racing Supplement* and *The Story Journal*.

In 1917 he became a Special Constable at Lincoln's Inn and also a special interrogator for the War Office. His first marriage to Ivy Caldecott, daughter of a missionary, had ended in divorce and he married his much younger secretary, Violet King.

The Daily Mail sent Wallace to investigate atrocities in the Belgian Congo, a trip that provided material for his *Sanders of the River* books. In 1923 he became Chairman of the Press Club and in 1931 stood as a Liberal candidate at Blackpool. On being offered a scriptwriting contract at RKO, Wallace went to Hollywood. He died in 1932, on his way to work on the screenplay for *King Kong*.

BY THE SAME AUTHOR
ALL PUBLISHED BY HOUSE OF STRATUS

THE ADMIRABLE CARFEW
THE ANGEL OF TERROR
THE AVENGER *(USA: THE HAIRY ARM)*
BARBARA ON HER OWN
BIG FOOT
THE BLACK ABBOT
BONES
BONES IN LONDON
BONES OF THE RIVER
THE CLUE OF THE NEW PIN
THE CLUE OF THE SILVER KEY
THE CLUE OF THE TWISTED CANDLE
THE COAT OF ARMS *(USA: THE ARRANWAYS MYSTERY)*
THE COUNCIL OF JUSTICE
THE CRIMSON CIRCLE
THE DAFFODIL MYSTERY
THE DARK EYES OF LONDON *(USA: THE CROAKERS)*
THE DAUGHTERS OF THE NIGHT
A DEBT DISCHARGED
THE DEVIL MAN
THE DOOR WITH SEVEN LOCKS
THE DUKE IN THE SUBURBS
THE FACE IN THE NIGHT
THE FEATHERED SERPENT
THE FLYING SQUAD
THE FORGER *(USA: THE CLEVER ONE)*
THE FOUR JUST MEN
FOUR SQUARE JANE
THE FOURTH PLAGUE
THE FRIGHTENED LADY
GOOD EVANS
THE HAND OF POWER
THE IRON GRIP
THE JOKER *(USA: THE COLOSSUS)*
THE JUST MEN OF CORDOVA
THE KEEPERS OF THE KING'S PEACE
THE LAW OF THE FOUR JUST MEN
THE LONE HOUSE MYSTERY
THE MAN WHO BOUGHT LONDON
THE MAN WHO KNEW
THE MAN WHO WAS NOBODY
THE MIND OF MR J G REEDER *(USA: THE MURDER BOOK OF J G REEDER)*
MORE EDUCATED EVANS
MR J G REEDER RETURNS *(USA: MR REEDER RETURNS)*
MR JUSTICE MAXELL
RED ACES
ROOM 13
SANDERS
SANDERS OF THE RIVER
THE SINISTER MAN
THE SQUARE EMERALD *(USA: THE GIRL FROM SCOTLAND YARD)*
THE THREE JUST MEN
THE THREE OAK MYSTERY
WHEN THE GANGS CAME TO LONDON

The Traitor's Gate

HOUSE OF STRATUS

This edition published in 2001 by House of Stratus, an imprint of
Stratus Books Ltd., 21 Beeching Park, Kelly Bray,
Cornwall, PL17 8QS, UK.

www.houseofstratus.com

Typeset, printed and bound by House of Stratus.

A catalogue record for this book is available from the British Library and the Library of Congress.

ISBN 07551-152-1-X

We would like to thank the Edgar Wallace Society for all the support they have given House of Stratus. Enquiries on how to join the Edgar Wallace Society should be addressed to:
The Edgar Wallace Society, c/o Penny Wyrd, 84 Ridgefield Road, Oxford, OX4 3DA.
Email: info@edgarwallace.org Web: http://www.edgarwallace.org/

TO MY DEAR FRIEND
DOROTHY DICKSON
("CORA ANN")

1

"Gua-a-ard! Slope – hime!"

Thirty-one rifles moved as one – thirty-one white hands came back to the seams of thirty-one trousers as though impelled by some invisible machinery. "Arms!" the word should have been; "hime" it was and had been since the beginning of military life. Motionless, the straight scarlet line stood, great bearskin headgears in perfect alignment. The march the band was playing came to its crashing, thunderous end as the last four of the old guard disappeared round the angle of the white tower.

"Dis-miss!"

Bobby Longfellow sent his slim sword into its scabbard with a "click," fixed his monocle more firmly in his eye, and glared at the squat little church of St Peter ad Vincula, bathed in the sunlight of a summer morning, and became dimly conscious of a short, stout lady who, guidebook in hand, had approached him. His sergeant stood rigidly by, wondering and, behind the mask of a teak-carved face, laughing silently.

"I beg your pardon, sir."

Bobby had seventy-five inches of elevation. The sound came from somewhere below him, and he looked down.

The stout lady wore a bonnet ornamented with gouts and slithers of jet, a beaded cape, and at her throat a large cameo brooch. Her face was big and hot and genial. She had, he noted, three chins and a rather masculine nose.

"Sorry – h'm!"

"Could you tell me where Lady Jane Grey is buried?"

She had a deep bass voice. He blinked at her like a man who had suddenly come into the light.

"Lady – ?"

"Lady Jane Grey, sir."

He looked helplessly at the sergeant; his white gloves fiddled with a meagre moustache.

"Have you – er – looked in the cemetery?" he asked hopefully.

"Which cemetery, sir?"

The sergeant gave no encouragement.

"Well – um – *any* cemetery! Do you know this lady, sergeant?"

"Never seen her before, sir."

Bobby made a clicking noise to signify the sergeant's error.

"Lady – what's her name again? – Grey."

The stout woman grew helpful.

"She's buried near the B – Tower," she said discreetly.

Bobby's white-gloved hand comprehended every building.

"This is all the B – Tower, isn't it, sergeant?" he asked bitterly.

The sergeant thought it was.

"Better inquire of a meat-eater – beefeater – ma'am."

He might have protested against the indignity offered to the officer of the guard, arrayed in all the panoply of war, by being mistaken for a guide, but somehow this never occurred to him. It was his first day's duty at the Tower, and he rather hated it. He hated the heat of the day, he loathed the tightly-fitting scarlet tunic and the perspiring bearskin. In fact, Lieutenant Robert Longfellow wished he was anything at that moment but a subaltern of His Majesty's Regiment of Berwick Guards.

The stout woman consulted her guidebook.

"Where's them Crown jew'ls kept, sir?"

"In the safe, dear old lady," said Bobby promptly.

Happily a real guide came along and, to his intense relief, piloted the visitor to the Wakefield Tower.

"How perfectly fearfully awful!" said Bobby. "What the deuce am I supposed to tell her, sergeant?"

"Nothing, sir," said the sergeant, and Bobby brightened.

He went into the guardroom and to his own private apartment, and Mrs Ollorby continued her sightseeing, though in truth this red-faced lady was interested neither in Crown jewels nor the unfortunate Jane whose head had been sliced from her frail body within a few yards of where she had asked her questions.

But there was a visitor to the Tower of London that morning who found a pathetic interest in Lady Jane's fate. Hope Joyner stood by the chain that protects the little square slab of sacrifice from sacrilegious feet, and looked down at the simple inscription and then across to the tiny church where the girl-wife was laid to rest.

"Poor – poor dear!" she said softly, and Richard Hallowell could not find the heart to smile.

For here was youth lamenting youth's passing; shingled beauty bent in sorrow over the spot where Jane's long hair had been brought over her head that the work of the axe might not be hampered. He could admire a profile as perfect as any he had seen, and a figure more gracious in its drooping tenderness than when it had stood as straight as a lance. Her colouring was soft and flawless against the grey background of age-blackened stones. Somehow the tragedy of Somerset's ambition grew more poignant and real in the presence of this vital expression of youthful womanhood.

"Yes – horrible, wasn't it? She lodged at the King's House... From that window she saw her husband carried past after his death... Hope, you are making the morning rather a sad one!"

She flashed a quick smile at him and dropped her hand on his arm.

"Then I'm a brute, Dick! I will be good – isn't that resplendent creature Bobbie?"

The lank form of the officer of the guard had appeared under the veranda of the guard-house.

"That is Bobbie. He came off leave last night and he is making his first acquaintance with Tower guard duty," he chuckled. "He's a born loafer – a little gentle work will do him the world of good!"

"That is the first time you have smiled today," she reproached him, and though he might have told her that he had little excuse for smiles that morning, he said nothing.

Dick Hallowell, in his black, perfectly fitting frock coat, girded about with the scarlet sash of rank, was a head taller than she – keen-faced, grey-eyed, he had something of the suppleness of the born athlete and something of an athlete's spring in his walk.

"And now I have shown you everything," he said. "I was hoping it would take the whole day."

She laughed softly.

"That isn't true! You've been fidgeting to get rid of me ever since your servant came to you. Somebody is waiting to see you?" Before he could answer she went on: "I'm a born sightseer, and besides, I know the Tower rather well. But I did so wish to see what you really were like in uniform?"

As she spoke, she realised with a sense of dismay how very short a time they had known one another. Less than a month before, a lost punt pole had brought them together in a shady backwater of the Thames, she drifting ridiculously to no worse fate than entanglement in an osier bed, and he canoeing to her rescue with no other sense than of amusement.

They paced down the slope towards the Lion Gate and stopped under the archway to gaze with one accord at the grim wooden barrier behind which was the river.

"Traitor's Gate!"

She shivered, though why she could not for the life of her understand.

"Traitor's Gate," he nodded. "A highly respectable gateway nowadays – you would never dream that queens and courtiers had trodden those steps. That is the place where Queen Elizabeth sat down and said she'd be damned if she went any farther!"

She laughed again and they went on, past the saluting sentries, until they came to the everyday world of Tower Hill, a place of huge trolleys laden with cases and a smell of fish from nearby Billingsgate.

Hope's big Rolls moved silently to the kerb, and Dick opened the door.

"I shall see you – when?"

She smiled at this.

"Just whenever you wish. I am a name in the telephone book and I like lunching at the Embassy!"

"What are you going to do now?"

She made a little face at this.

"I've an unpleasant interview ahead of me," she said, and he stared at her. And so had he – but this much he did not confess.

He watched the car out of sight before he turned, strode down the hill, across the bridge that spans the ancient moat. And he was smiling no more. Not even the mute and pathetic appeal for sympathy that Bobbie made to him as he passed the guardroom moved the troubled frown from his good-looking face.

At the entrance to his quarters Brill, his servant, was waiting.

"The gentleman told me to go out and see if I could find you, sir – he says he has an appointment."

Dick Hallowell nodded slowly.

"I shan't need you for a quarter of an hour, Brill," he said. "You had better stay here, and if anybody wants me, tell them that I am very busy."

"Yes, Sir Richard."

"And, Brill, did – er – the gentleman say anything to you…about himself?"

Brill hesitated.

"No, sir. He seemed a bit short of temper, and said that you ought to be glad to have quarters like these – "

Again he hesitated.

"Yes?"

"That's all, sir…he sort of sneered. I thought it was cheek, sir. His coming here and criticising. He's nothing so far as I can see."

"Yes – nothing."

Dick went up the stone stairs, stopped at the door on a landing, and with a grimace pushed open the door and walked in. Standing by the window of the comfortable sitting room, and apparently absorbed in the spectacle of a drill squad, stood a man. His face, half turned towards Dick, was thin and discontented, his clothes shabby, his boots down at heel. Yet in face and carriage there was a peculiar likeness to the silent, watchful officer.

"Hallo!"

He turned with a growl to the contemplation of his host, and his scrutiny was neither friendly nor without offence.

"Hallo – brother!"

Dick said nothing. As they faced one another the likeness was more observable, and yet there was a distinct dissimilarity. Had Graham Hallowell eradicated the harshness from his voice, it would have been identical; but he had forgotten the art of amiability, forgotten that he had ever captained the boats at a great school, and been the pride and ornament of a university. All that he knew was that he was a hardly used man, a man who had "never had a chance"; he had reached the stage where he could remember only his grievances and the sour happenings of life.

"Your welcome is as enthusiastic as ever – Sir Richard!" he sneered. "And I'll bet that you aren't going to ask me to lunch in the mess, eh? 'Meet my brother – Graham Hallowell – he came out of Dartmoor yesterday and he will be able to tell you some most amusing stories of Naked Hell!' "

His voice rose until it was almost a shout. Dick realised that he had been drinking and was in his most poisonous mood.

"Even your damned servant treats me as though I were a leper – "

"You are!" Dick Hallowell's tone was subdued and crystal-clear. "A leper – that describes you, Graham! Something foul that self-respecting people wish to avoid. Something inhuman without a quality acceptable to God or man. And don't shout when you talk to me, or I'll take you by the scruff of the neck and kick you down the stairs. Is that clear?"

The man seemed to cower at the threat. From the hectoring bully he became the wailing suppliant.

"Don't take any notice of me, Dick – I've had two over the eight this morning, old man. Imagine how you would feel if you had been released from prison only yesterday – put yourself in my place – "

He was interrupted.

"I can't imagine how I should feel when I qualified for prison," said the other coldly. "I haven't that much imagination. It is impossible to put myself in your place when you drugged and robbed a foolish young officer of the Guards who trusted you because you were my half-brother. It is impossible to visualise myself running away with a decent man's wife and leaving her to starve in Vienna. There are other things I can't imagine – I need not describe them in detail. When I can put myself in your place, so that I can understand just how a man can grovel in the mud as you have grovelled, I shall be better able to share your emotions at finding yourself at liberty. What do you want?"

Graham's restless eyes sought the window.

"I'm broke," he said sullenly. "I thought of getting away to America – "

"Have the American police discovered a shortage of blackguards, that you need go to America?"

"You're hard as hell, Dick."

Dick Hallowell laughed – it was not the laughter of amusement.

"How much do you want?"

"Well, the fare to New York – "

"They will not admit you to the United States with your record – you know that."

"I could take another name" – eagerly.

"You will not go – you have no intention of going."

Dick sat down at his desk, opened a drawer and, taking out a cheque book, wrote.

"I have made this for fifty pounds, and I have written it so that it will be impossible for you to alter the sum to five hundred, as you did with the last cheque I gave you. Moreover, I shall take the precaution of calling my bank on the telephone and notifying them the amount."

He tore out the cheque and handed it to the scowling visitor.

"And that is the last money you will get from me. If you imagine that you can force me by coming here and raising Cain, you have another guess coming. My colonel and my brother officers know all about you – the boy you swindled is on guard at this very moment. If you trouble me I will lock you up. Is that clear also?"

Graham Hallowell slipped the cheque into his pocket.

"You're like a bit of stone," he whined. "If father knew – "

"Thank God he is dead!" said Dick soberly. "But he knew enough to die of a broken heart. I've got that against you, Graham."

Graham breathed heavily. Only fear held down the fury that flamed in his breast. He wanted to hurt – to lacerate – to humble this well-hated half-brother of his, and he lacked the courage.

"Through the window I saw you talking to a beauteous maiden – "

"Be silent!" snapped Dick. "I will not have you discuss any lady with me."

"Hoity-toity!" He was recovering a little of his old insolence. "I was merely asking – does Diana know?"

Dick walked to the door and flung it wide open.

"That is your way," he said tersely.

"Diana – "

"Diana is nothing to me. Will you remember that? I don't like her friends for one thing."

"Meaning me?"

His brother nodded to the staircase, and with a shrug the man swaggered past.

"This place is like a prison – but I'll find my way out."

"The best way out for you is locked and barred," Richard Hallowell smiled grimly.

"What's that?"

"The Traitor's Gate!" said Dick, and slammed the door on him.

2

The telephone bell rang for the third time; it conveyed a sense of impatience. Diana Montague deposited the fluffy little Pom on a cushion and reached out lazily for the instrument. It was Colley, of course, querulous, rather inclined to waste time in bewailing the length of time she had kept him waiting.

"Had we known it was your serene highness, we should have leapt to the first tinkle," said Diana ominously. It sounded ominous to Colley, who hated sarcastic women.

"Can you meet me at Ciro's for lunch?" he asked.

"No; we cannot meet you anywhere for lunch," she answered. "I am lunching here with Mr Graham Hallowell."

Evidently the news was a surprise to him.

"Hallowell? I really can't hear you distinctly, Diana; are you smoking?"

She blew a grey cloud to the ceiling, tapped the ash of her cigarette into the crystal tray.

"No," she said, "but I am a little inarticulate this morning. The prospect of being alone with a gentleman who has just come out of prison is a little overpowering.

He doesn't run true to type, Colley. In the first place, he wasn't wrongly convicted – "

"Listen, Di – "

"Don't call me Di!" she interrupted angrily.

"Diana. The Big Fellow wants to meet you – honest. He said so."

"Tell the Big Fellow that I don't wish to meet him," she said, calmly again. "One criminal a day is quite enough thrill."

He was silent for a second. Then:

"Oh, say! Being funny, aren't you? I don't believe that you *are* lunching with Hallowell!"

She put the receiver down on the table and resumed her book. When Colley Warrington was rude or trying she invariably put the receiver on the table and just let it buzz.

And Colley could be very trying. He was occasionally in love with her and as occasionally he fell into violent jealousies. He was in love with her just now and she was rather bored.

A soft tap at the door: Dombret came in with a swish of her taffeta skirts – Diana invariably dressed her maids in purple taffeta and insisted upon musical comedy aprons and teashop head-dresses. Dombret, being twenty and pretty, carried taffeta well, and the high cap gave her something of the appearance of a Russian Madonna.

"Would you see Miss Joyner, mademoiselle?"

"Miss Joyner!" Diana stared at the maid. "Are you sure – Miss Joyner?"

"Yes, ma'm'selle. A very pretty young lady."

Diana thought quickly.

"Ask her to come up, please."

Dombret was out of the room a few seconds.

"Miss Joyner."

Diana crossed the floor, one hand out-thrown, a dazzling smile on her normally pale face. She knew just exactly how she looked, being self-conscious in the confident sense of the phrase, and well aware of her perfect lines and the red splendour of her hair.

"This is most delightful of you, Miss Joyner."

Hope Joyner took the hand, her clear grey eyes met Diana's in a look that was neither antagonistic nor suspicious. She was three years the younger, at the age when it is difficult to remember just what she looked like a year ago; when girlhood had acquired a certain mystery and reticence and the lank body that could only be guessed behind loose-fitting jumpers is formless no more.

"I wondered if you would mind my calling," she said.

So this was Hope Joyner? She was lovely. Diana was a hard critic, most difficult to please, but she found nothing to criticise in shape or voice or colouring.

"I'm *awfully* pleased – sit down, won't you?"

She grabbed the drowsy little dog from the couch; he protested shrilly and was cuffed to silence. Cuffs and pettings were the alternates of Togo's experience. But Hope remained standing, one white hand resting on the billowy end of the couch.

"I had a letter from you – rather a curious letter," she said. "May I read it – perhaps you have forgotten what you said."

Diana never forgot such things, but she offered no objection, watching the girl with a detached interest as she opened her handbag, took out an envelope and produced from the cover a sheet of heavy grey notepaper. Without preamble, she began to read:

DEAR MISS JOYNER,
I trust you will not think it impertinent of me to write to you on a matter which touches me very closely, and I know enough of you to believe that you will respect my confidence. Briefly, I am in this embarrassing position. Until you appeared on the scene I was engaged to be married to Sir Richard Hallowell – although just now we are estranged on a family matter which would not interest you. You have been seen about with him very frequently of late and people are talking rather unkindly about you – asking who you are, where you come from, what is your family. That, however, concerns me –

She stopped to turn over the closely written sheet.

– concerns me less than my own prospects of happiness. I love Dick very dearly and he loves me, though for the moment we are scarcely on speaking terms. Might I not appeal to your generosity and ask you to give us the opportunity of renewing our friendship?

She finished reading, restored the letter to her bag and closed it gently.

"I don't think that is an unreasonable request," said Diana coolly.

"That I should obliterate myself?" asked Hope in her quiet, incisive way. "But why should I? You have all the opportunities you need, and aren't you presuming a great deal?"

Diana bit her lip thoughtfully.

"Perhaps I am – it was a silly letter, but I was distracted. Of course, it doesn't mean because you're a friend, that you care for him – "

Hope shook her head.

"I didn't mean that. What I intended was to ask you whether you weren't presuming an enormous capacity for sacrifice on my part?"

Diana's eyes narrowed.

"You mean – that you love him?"

Hope Joyner nodded. Her eyes did not waver.

"That is what I mean," she said.

The confession took Diana's breath away, and it was some time before she recovered her voice.

"How very touching!" she said, but Hope Joyner was impervious to the sneer. "So I presume that my very reasonable request to you will not affect your" – she paused deliberately – "ambitious plan?"

"Is it very ambitious?" asked Hope, with a certain baffling innocence. "I mean, to like or love Dick Hallowell?"

Diana kept a tight hold of herself. She had not expected much good to come from her letter; indeed, the writing of it had been the merest whimsical impulse. Perhaps she had wanted to hurt Dick Hallowell, to annoy him. And now, facing the girl, so radiant in her beauty, so confident in her love, she saw a challenge in the girl's very presence; in the unwavering, unfearing steadfastness of her eyes – and Diana was a bad person to challenge.

It was curious how, in that moment, all the dead resentment came to life, and the dead ashes of rage which had consumed her four years ago glowed red and hotly. Across bleak skies showed the blurred shadow of might-have-beens… Hope saw her swallow, saw the teeth meet even as Diana smiled.

"I will show you something."

The voice that spoke was strange even to Diana, yet it was her own. She was gone from the room for a few seconds and came back holding between finger and thumb a small leather case. Snapping open the catch, the lid flew back and revealed a ring of three brilliant diamonds. Slipping the ring from its support, she thrust it into Hope's unwilling hands.

"Will you read what is inside, please?"

Mechanically the girl obeyed, though she was not very curious. Engraved on the inside of the lid were the words: "Dick to Diana, 1922."

Hope handed the ring back to the woman.

"Well?" demanded Diana.

"An engagement ring?"

The other woman nodded. Hope was looking at her, puzzled.

"Does it really – affect the situation?" she asked. "Is that a more convincing argument than any you have used why I should not see Richard Hallowell? I know you were engaged to him: he told me – at least, he told me he was engaged to – somebody. Most people are engaged more than once, aren't they? Honestly, Miss Martyn, I don't know whether I'm being a cat or whether I'm just being awfully sane, but do you seriously expect me not to see Richard Hallowell again?"

"I expect you to do as you please." Diana's voice was almost tart. "Obviously," with a shrug, "it is a matter of taste and good breeding. You cannot expect me to think for you."

Her eyes were on her bag.

"Perhaps it was an indiscreet letter to write," she said, and held out her hand. "May I have it back, please?"

Again their eyes met, and then, opening the bag, Hope took out the letter, tore it in four pieces and put the scraps of paper upon the table. With a nod she turned and left the room, so unexpectedly that the inquisitive Dombret, with her ear glued to the keyhole, almost fell in the room as she opened the door. Diana walked to the window to catch another glimpse of her as she left the house, but was unsuccessful.

Why on earth – ?

Diana Martyn was puzzled at herself; could not construe her own motives. She had given up all thought of Dick Hallowell years before – he was as remote a factor as any in her life. She tried to remember just why the letter had been written. There was a streak of impishness in Diana Martyn, a curious perversity of reasoning which had led her before into many minor and one great scrape. She did not like to think about this letter, for it had to do with Dick Hallowell. She had written the letter mischievously, never doubting that Hope would show it to the man most interested, expecting from Dick one of those storming epistles of which he was capable; she had certainly never expected the appearance in her exquisite drawing-room of this girl with her calm, provocative beauty.

She was trying to get in order the basic causes of her present emotions, when Dombret came into the room to announce a caller, who followed on her heels. Diana was sitting on one of the broad window-seats that commanded a view of Curzon Street, her arms folded, one white finger at her lips; and now she scrutinised critically, unmercifully, the shabby man who strode in, a scowl on his face, his hands thrust in his pockets. Waiting until the door closed on Dombret, she asked:

"Why?"

"Why what?" he demanded roughly.

"Why this general threadbareness?"

Graham Hallowell looked down at his soiled clothing and grinned.

"I forgot to change," he said.

She nodded slowly.

"So you've been to see the great Richard – and was the great Richard duly impressed by the evidence of your poverty?"

He dropped down on the big settee, took a paper packet of cigarettes from his pocket, and lit one, making no reply.

"Is there any particular reason why you should appear in Curzon Street got up like a scarecrow – I at any rate am not impressed."

"Neither was he," he said, puffing a cloud of smoke to the ceiling and watching it dissolve. "He gave me a mouldy fifty. I nearly chucked it at him."

"But you didn't quite," she said.

He had long ceased to be irritated by the undercurrent of sarcasm in her tone; it was part of her mental and moral make-up. There was a time when these subtle sneers of hers enraged him to the point of madness. But that was long ago.

"I suppose," she said thoughtfully, "you banked on his paying you any sum you asked in order to get rid of you, and of course he didn't! I wish you knew Dick as well as I."

"I know him too well," he growled. "The Pharisaical swine!"

She delayed her answer to this for a considerable time, her white teeth working at her lower lip.

"Pharisaical? No! Dick isn't a Pharisee." After a pause: "I suppose he didn't mention me?"

"He said he didn't want to hear about you, if that is any satisfaction."

She nodded.

"Which means that you did the speaking."

"He's got a new girl," broke in Graham, "and she's a beauty! I saw them draping themselves sentimentally over the execution place."

She did not appear to be interested, and, looking round the apartment, he framed the question that he would have asked the previous night, but his nerve had failed him, for he stood in some awe of this woman.

"You've got a beautiful place, Diana. I'm not especially curious, but I'm wondering how it is done. If I remember rightly, you were living in furnished rooms when I went away. I noticed your change of address, but this magnificence is rather staggering."

She had, as he knew, an income of a few hundreds a year, barely sufficient to pay the rent of this apartment. She wrote a little, was on excellent terms with Fleet Street, but her natural indolence made this source of revenue a meagre one. She smiled a little sourly.

"You fear the worst? Well, you need not. I am being rather industrious just now. Have you heard of the Prince of Kishlastan?"

He shook his head.

"You haven't?" She waved her hand around the room. "Behold his largesse!"

She laughed at the look of consternation that came to his face.

"I'm his press agent," she said coolly. "That doesn't sound a very high-class job, but it has been worth the better part of four thousand a year to me, and I think I've earned my money. The Prince has a grievance against the world, and against the Government in particular. Colley Warrington introduced him to me two years ago. I think he'd been trying to bleed our friend, who, by the way, is painfully rich, and had failed, and he thought of working me in as a sideline, and of course I was terribly sympathetic with his excellency, and it didn't take very long to discover the chinks in his golden armour. He has lost two guns – "

"Two what?" asked the puzzled Graham.

"Two guns," she said. "Apparently the French governor allowed our friend to be saluted with nine rounds of blank cartridge, but he got into some trouble, there was a scandal of sorts, and the salute was reduced to seven. You wouldn't think it possible that that sort of thing would bother a grown man, but it's evidently a terribly important matter in India. And he's a lunatic on the question of precious stones. He has the most wonderful collection in India."

"Is he married?" asked Graham suspiciously.

"Nine deep," she replied calmly. "I haven't met any of his wives; they are kept strictly purdah – that is the term, I believe. I really have been very useful to him – I've interested our ambassador in Paris, and I've written or inspired innumerable articles about him."

He was looking at her suspiciously, fingering his chin. She laughed.

"You have an East-is-East-and-West-is-West look in your eyes, Graham," she said, "and I have a feeling that you're going to develop into one of your censor-of-behaviour moods."

"It is queer, that's all," he said, and lit a cigar.

Her attitude was not friendly; he felt that. Presently he threw the cigar into the fireplace with a curse.

"I'll go home and change," he growled as he rose. "And this press agent business – I'm not so sure that I like it, Diana."

"That will hardly keep me awake," she answered coolly. "I suppose you realise that the four hundred pounds a year which was once mine is mine no longer. In a moment of mad optimism I loaned the capital to a young gentleman with a great scheme for getting rich quick – incidentally, I lost a perfectly good fiancé."

Her tone was light, but there was an underlying sourness in the words, and he shifted uneasily.

"You'll get all that back. I get twenty thousand on my next birthday."

"So you said before," she bantered him; "and there is your mother's will to prove it! Unfortunately, you've already mortgaged that legacy, as I discovered after you went to prison." And then, with a change of voice: "Go home and get into respectable clothes, and be back by one o'clock." She glanced at the jewelled watch on her wrist. "You haven't much time – hurry! I am expecting Colley to call. If he finds you are not here he will think I have been lying to him."

She walked with him to the door of the room and closed it after him, a little too soon for his dignity, and with a grimace she came back to the couch and was apparently absorbed in the newest and the most hectic of novels when Colley was announced.

Colley Warrington was a painfully thin man with a painfully narrow head, sparsely covered with yellow hair in quantities hardly sufficient to hide his incipient baldness. His face was long and furrowed, he had the appearance of a man who was prematurely old. People who hastily generalised called him dissipated, and wondered where the money came from to dissipate at all.

There are in London, in New York – indeed, in every centre of society the world holds – a sprinkling of men who make all people's business their own. Especially those people whose names are to be found in those volumes devoted to *haut ton*.

Colley knew everybody – could without reference to any guide-book rattle off their titles to greatness, who were their mothers and other relations, even to the remotest cousins, so long as the remote cousins had also some claim to importance. He knew their incomes to an *n*th, the state of repair or disrepair in which their properties stood. Walk Bond Street with him and you had comedy and tragedy at your elbow, for in the common objects he saw a significance beyond the ken of the average.

"...Lily Benerley in her Rolls – a fellow at the Egyptian Embassy gave her that – a fearful outsider. There's old Lady Vannery, drinks like a fish but she's got half a million; her nephew, Jack Wadser, inherits it when she pegs out – he married Mildred Perslow – the girl who ran away to Kenya with Leigh Castol, Lord Mensem's son..."

Uncharitable folks hinted that Colley found his instinct for scandal a source of profit "crook-bred and crook-minded" a certain Lord Chancellor had described him, not inaptly. There had been some sort of scandal at the Paddock Club – a card-room dispute. Colley had resigned quietly. There was no fuss. He was on the fringe of the Torkinton blackmail case, and found it convenient to rusticate at Aix-en-Provence whilst the trial was in progress. No reference was made to him by name in court, but when a learned counsel asked: "There was, I believe, Another Person in your confidence when you wrote those threatening letters?" everybody knew who Another Person was.

Such a man was Colley Warrington, who came scowling into the drawing-room and stood gloomily surveying Diana.

" 'Lo, Diana!"

There was no extraordinary enthusiasm in the greeting.

"Sit down and don't scowl."

"Where's Graham?" he asked.

"Gone home to change."

He seated himself carefully on the edge of a chair and lifted his perfectly creased trousers, displaying a pair of white silk socks above the polished radiance of his enamelled shoes.

"You're a fool to have anything to do with Graham – you know his reputation."

"He knows yours," she answered with a half smile; "and I gather that your views as to who is, and who is not, a desirable companion, have something in common with Graham's, except that he feels that you are the man of all men that no decent woman could be seen around with."

Colley said something under his breath.

"Don't swear, don't be bad-tempered; I want to ask you something. You're an encyclopaedia, Colley, and I've never consulted you before. Who is Hope Joyner?"

His ruling passion was strong enough to obliterate his ill temper.

"Hope Joyner?" he repeated. "That's the girl with a big flat in Devonshire House, isn't it? She has two cars, a Rolls and a big Yankee car; pots of money, and she is a friend of Dick Hallowell's..."

"I know all about that," she said impatiently; "but who is she?"

He shook his head.

"I don't know. She sort of appeared from nowhere. Went to a good school, I believe – one of those swagger establishments at Ascot, where lineage is spelt with a £. It's queer you should be interested in her! I was only talking about her the other day to Bobbie Longfellow, the Guardsman – "

"I didn't know you were a friend of his," interrupted Diana quickly.

"I'm not," he admitted frankly; "but even one's enemies talk. She's an orphan; her father was a Chilian, who left her all his fortune. It's administered by Roke & Morty, and why Roke & Morty should be trusted to administer an estate of that kind the Lord knows."

She frowned at this; the name was unfamiliar, and he went on to explain.

"They're criminal lawyers – almost crooks themselves, I believe, but they're in most of the big cases that come to the Old Bailey. If a fellow gets into bad trouble they're the people to engage."

"What is her history?" asked Diana, cutting short an interesting biography of these legal gentlemen.

"Blest if I know." Colley rubbed his thinly covered head. "She used to live at Monk's Chase, a property down in Berkshire. Rather a nice old house; it goes back to the last Henry…"

"For God's sake don't talk architecture to me, or I'll scream!" said Diana.

"Anyway, she used to live there," Colley went on, anxious to appease one who had before exhibited a gift for unpleasant repartee. "She was under the charge of a man called Hallett, an old gentleman. I think she must have been there for years. Hallett was in America most of the time, and the girl was under the care of his housekeeper. When she left Monk's Chase she went to school, and from school to Paris for a finishing course. She's always had money, stacks of it! Roke & Morty fixed up the flat for her; that's all I know. Why are you so infernally interested?"

Diana blew a long spiral of smoke from her lips before she replied.

"I am interested," she said, "because this young and charming lady has to be scientifically but effectively suppressed."

Colley stared in astonishment, then grinned.

"She is going to take a lot of suppressing, my dear, and there's a man in London who is mad crazy about her."

"I know," she interrupted roughly. "Dick Hallowell."

"Dick Hallowell!" he scoffed. "I'm not thinking about him."

It was her turn to be astonished.

"Whom do you mean? Who is in love with her?"

Colley was inclined to be theatrical; he was theatrical now, and he struck an attitude.

"Our exalted master and friend, His Excellency the Prince of Kishlastan."

The Prince! Diana did not believe him; thought he was indulging in an ill-timed jest.

"But he doesn't know her," she said.

Colley nodded.

"He has seen her, my dear, and to see is to love, as the poet says. He goes down to the Row regularly every morning to watch her ride; pays people to discover what theatre she goes to, so that he can sit in a box and gloat over her; thinks almost as much of her as he does of his precious guns and his quarter-mile of pearls. And tonight he's meeting her."

"Tonight? How – at the reception?" she asked quickly.

Colley nodded.

"The reception is arranged especially to afford Riki a chance of meeting his divinity. Why else do you think? He hates the English, and would no more think of giving a party than I should think of paying for one. He got to know Hope by the simple process of interesting her in the Oriental Women's Association. You know the kind of bunk – save our brown sisters from the horrors of polygamy. It is a very simple matter to get to know any girl you like."

Diana rose and walked slowly up and down the room, her hands clasped behind her.

"He has said nothing to me," she repeated.

"Why should he?" drawled Colley. "After all, men do not as a rule consult their – press agents about their love affairs."

"You're very crude," said Diana.

She walked to the door, intending to go to her bedroom to get a handkerchief. As she turned the handle and threw the door open, she stood petrified with astonishment.

Standing outside was a stout, middle-aged woman with a big frame and a powerful nose, and two eyes that twinkled with amusement.

"Who – who are you?" gasped Diana.

"Good morning, ma'am. My name's Ollorby."

She fumbled in her bag, took out a large card and handed it to the girl, who was too astonished even to examine the pasteboard.

"I've got a servants' agency. Any time you want a maid or a cook, I'll be glad if you'll ring me up. Three-seven-nine-four Soho…"

"How did you get in?" demanded Diana and then her anger rising: "How dare you come into this flat without permission?"

She looked round for Dombret.

"It's my fault entirely," said Mrs Ollorby, almost humbly. "The door was open, and I couldn't make anyone hear, so I just walked in. Any time you're in want of a servant – "

"I don't want a servant and I don't want you!" Diana pointed to the outer door of the flat, and in no wise abashed, Mrs Ollorby walked out with a briskness that was unexpected in one of her years. Diana slammed the door and went back to Colley.

"What's the trouble?" he asked lazily.

"A wretched servants' agent!"

She rang the bell furiously, and after a while Dombret came in.

"How dare you leave the door open?"

"But I didn't, madam," protested the maid.

"Don't lie!" stormed Diana, "You left the door open and a wretched woman wandered in – heaven knows how long she was waiting…"

The providential arrival of Graham cut short the indignant Dombret's ordeal. Thereafter Diana dismissed the pushful agent from her mind and throughout lunch discussed mainly one topic – the Prince of Kishlastan and his passion for gewgaws, material and human.

3

There were those who thought that His Excellency the Prince of Kishlastan lacked something more than a sense of discretion. A tall, thin man, with the facial characteristics of the typical Easterner, he was for the moment not only under the ban of the French Government, but was extremely unpopular with the Government of India. Though nominally a French subject, since he took his title from a small patch of territory which impinged upon French possessions – a territory he so misruled that he had been brought before the Governor of Pondicherry – he had, to the embarrassment of the British Government, acquired vast estates in British India.

"Riki," as they called him, came to London with a confused grievance; and since he was a man of enormous wealth, found many sympathisers in that stratum of society which is ready to excuse the eccentricities of native rulers.

He was a daily visitor to the Row, an indefatigable first-nighter, and his dinner parties were marked by a luxury and profusion which had no exact parallel amongst the season's entertainments. It is true that no official from the Foreign Office attended these functions, that he was not to be met with in the circles associated with the official world; but though it withheld its countenance, yet, in a remote fashion the Foreign Office was inevitably represented on Riki's more elaborate occasions.

Dick Hallowell received a card of invitation to the reception which His Excellency was to hold, and at the same time he was privately notified that his presence at Arrid's Hotel would not be unfavourably regarded by the powers that be. Dick had spent four years of his childhood in India, had acquired a working knowledge of Hindustani which had been improved through his love of the language. He was in India acting as aide de camp to the Governor-General of Bengal when his father's death had brought him home to assume the responsibilities of the title and the task of settling up an estate which was in some ways slightly involved.

He strolled into Bobbie Longfellow's room, and found that lanky young man reclining in a deep chair, engrossed in the study of a sporting newspaper.

"Good Lord, you poor old soul!" said Bobbie when he read the card; and then his jaw dropping: "But you don't want me to meet that mad devil again, do you?"

Dick smiled.

"I don't know why you call him 'mad'. But I did think it would be an idea if you came along. I shall be bored stiff."

"Mad!" scoffed Bobbie. "Of course he's nutty! Why, I'd hardly put my foot in this castellated slum before I was told off to show him round the Jewel House. I don't know the Jewel House from a chicken run, but one of those ancient birds in the ridiculous uniform of Elizabeth – what do you call 'em, meat-eaters?"

"Beefeaters," said Dick.

Bobbie nodded.

One of those old creatures put me right, and I had to totter up those ghastly stairs and show him the royal jewels – I'd never seen 'em myself, so it really wasn't so bad."

"Why do you call him mad?" asked Dick.

Bobby nodded vigorously.

"He's mad on the question of jewels. Simply couldn't tear him away from the crown. He just hung on to the rails and glared at it. The things he said to the other Indian were terribly interesting, only I didn't understand them. He spoke in Hindustani. Wish you had been there, Dick. One of his people told me that he's crazy about diamonds, that he's got, in a room in Kishlastan, stones you couldn't buy for ten million sterling! And when he came out of the Jewel Tower, he was so upset that he was as limp as a rag. He wanted to give me two pearl earrings as a souvenir, but I told him, 'My dear rajah, I've given up wearing earrings – they haven't been fashionable for years.' "

Dick laughed softly.

"Anyway, you're going to be a good boy and come along to Arrid's tonight," he said. "I've had a request to be civil to His Excellency, and we needn't be there more than half an hour."

Bobbie groaned, threw his paper on to the nearest settee and drew his long form erect.

"Shall I wear my pearl necklace or my ruby bangle?" he demanded sardonically. "And I'd fixed to go to a theatre with one of the sweetest little things – "

"You can still go," said Dick. "We shan't be at Arrid's more than half an hour."

When they arrived that night at the hotel they found the broad stairway leading up to the first floor crowded with a brilliant and slowly moving throng. All that was nearly great in London was there: Members of Parliament, ex-Cabinet Ministers who represented a party not likely to return to office for many years and therefore enabled to show themselves without compromise to their principles, ladies who appeared everywhere except at Court, elderly Indian officers (themselves with grievances), a journalist, a writer or two – these they recognised as they progressed with the throng.

"There's Diana Martyn," said Bobbie suddenly, and Dick, looking up, saw her on the landing above, leaning on the balustrade and talking to Colley Warrington. As he made to pass her she favoured him with a smile and a cool little nod.

"This is an unexpected pleasure, Dick," she said, very self-possessed.

It was difficult even for Dick to believe that he had once been engaged to this calm and beautiful girl, or that their parting had ever been a tragedy to him. He could meet her without embarrassment, could even be mildly admiring, for in her jade dress, with a chain of big emeralds about her throat, her perfect skin and grave eyes, she was as beautiful a woman as a man might hope to meet in the course of a day's march through Mayfair.

"You're not married yet?" She smiled her inquiry.

"Not yet," he answered with perfect gravity.

"A little bird whispers that you contemplate – " She did not complete the sentence.

"Your little bird for once speaks truth," he said, meeting her challenge.

"How perfectly wonderful!" she murmured, and in another second they were separated, as he pushed forward to the open doors of the salon where His Excellency met his guests.

They cleared the fringe of people at the door, and then Dick halted, struck dumb with astonishment. In the centre of the room stood the rajah in an amethyst silken robe, girt at the waist with a broad sash of silver, and about his neck rope upon rope of pearls; but it was not the magnificence of the Easterner that transfixed the visitor.

Talking to him was a slim girl in white. Her back was turned to Dick, but he recognised her instantly.

"Good Lord!" gasped Bobbie. "That's your Hope, isn't it?"

"I don't know what you mean about 'my Hope,' " said Dick, with unnecessary irritation. "It *is* Miss Joyner, I think."

At that moment she turned her head and greeted him with a smile as he advanced to make his stiff obeisance to the Indian.

"It is delightful of you to come, Sir Richard," said the Prince in his mincing way, the lazy, heavy-lidded eyes surveying Dick with no especial favour. "I hoped to see you when I was at the Tower, but it was my misfortune that you were away. Do you know Miss Joyner?"

Dick smiled at the girl.

"An old friend – yes?" said the Prince, with just a hint of suspicion in his voice. "You are greatly privileged."

Another name was announced. Dick drew the girl from the circle, to the rajah's annoyance.

"What on earth are you doing in this galley?" he asked in amazement, and she laughed softly.

"I'm one of the world's workers: didn't you know that, Dick?" she replied. "I'm in the Oriental Woman's movement, though I can't say that I'm far in it. Lady Silford asked me to join her committee."

Dick knew Lady Silford very well for a woman with inordinate social ambitions and with a most meagre income to support them. She was by repute one of the many subsidised by this wealthy Indian, and he could have no doubt in his mind that though Lady Silford had issued the invitation, she had acted according to instructions. For a second he was a little perturbed, for he knew something of the rajah's private reputation.

"I don't think I should have much to do with these so-called movements," he said. "There are quite a number of genuine societies that are doing really good work, but the Oriental Woman's Association is a fake – so much so that the police refuse permission to make collections on its behalf."

"I'm not terribly interested," she confessed as they strolled towards the door.

Outside in the broad corridor they came face to face with Diana, and Diana greeted the girl with all the aplomb and enthusiasm which a close and lifelong friendship might excuse.

"Why, it is our little Hope!" she bantered. "And is this the – 'contemplation,' Dick?

It was Hope who saved him the embarrassment of replying.

"I saw you as I came up the stairs, but hadn't a chance to speak to you, Miss Martyn," she said. "I wanted to give you something."

She opened her jewelled bag and took out a flat leather case.

"This came to me by special messenger just before I left Devonshire House," she said. "The rajah's card is inside, but I thought some mistake had been made, and that perhaps you would rectify it for me. Will you?"

Diana took the package reluctantly.

"I don't know what it's all about," she began. "What is this?"

"A string of pearls," said the girl quietly. "Would you tell His Excellency that it isn't customary in England for a lady to receive presents – even from princes of the Golden East?"

Dick saw the tell-tale flush come to Diana's cheeks.

"Why should I be your messenger?"

"Because" – Hope was smiling – "you will find the rajah's card inside. My address is written upon it – in your handwriting!"

"Wait a moment!"

Diana's voice was hard: she put out her hand to detain the girl as she was moving off.

"I don't see why on earth you shouldn't accept a little present, if His Excellency deigns to favour you. After all" – her shrug was almost imperceptible – "you aren't anybody particular – forgive me if I'm frank – are you? I mean, one doesn't find your name in the landed gentry or in Debrett or in any of those useful books of reference."

"Nor in Carlow's List," said Hope coolly, and Diana went an angry red.

She left Diana standing with a fixed smile, but in her eyes a malignity which Dick had only seen once before.

"Who on earth is Carlow?" he demanded, when they were clear of the crowd.

"Didn't you know?" she asked innocently. "Carlow's is a big commercial agency, and they issue a list, very confidential and secret, to their clients – I am one of them. The List contains the names of everybody in England, and in London especially, who live by their wits and have been associated with criminals."

Dick gasped.

"What an extraordinary girl you are!"

"Aren't I?" she smiled, though she had never felt less like smiling in her life. "But then, I'm in rather an extraordinary position."

She refused his escort and drove home alone. Her mind was in a turmoil, for Diana Martyn had put into words all the uneasy, fretful questions she had been asking herself for the past five years.

She was "nobody" – Diana had spoken the truth. Beyond the fact that her parents were dead, that she had interests in South America, and was in receipt of a princely income paid regularly into her bank every quarter day by a firm of lawyers, who, even she knew, dealt with the shadiest of folk, she had no clue to her own identity.

She had never seen her own birth certificate, nor even knew in what country she had first seen the light of day. The mysterious Mr Hallett might have told her, but Mr Hallett she had never met with. She knew nothing about him except that he was an elderly man who travelled a great deal, and whose eyesight had been failing ever since she could remember. Yet she had lived in Mr Hallett's house for years; had come there on her vacation from school; had enjoyed the run of his estate, the use of his horses, the respect and care of his servants.

A restless man, who seemed to be travelling all the time, now in India, now in America, now in Southern Europe, she had almost come to regard him as the symbol of all that was baffling in her life. Sometimes she hated him. He never answered the letters she wrote, had never addressed one kind word to her. Presents had come on her birthday, at Christmas, flowers invariably reached her on the tenth day of June of every year, but not a line of his writing had she seen. He was a man who was doing his duty mechanically, without any great heartiness, she felt, and always avoiding her. She was certain that it was no coincidence that he left Monk's Chase the day before she reached there on her summer vacation, and returned a few days after she left. Her letters to him were answered by his banker, of all people in the world, a stuffy old man who lived in a dingy office in Threadneedle Street, and who was no more interested in her than Mr Hallett himself.

As her maid undressed her that night her mind was fixed on Monk's Chase, and the little cupboard in the library which a garrulous Nannie had once pointed out as containing all the secrets that she desired to unravel. Was it invention on the old woman's part to amuse or quieten her, or was it possible that in that cupboard –

In a moment of childish adventure she had sought all the keys she could discover for one that would unlock the cupboard; had actually discovered such a key and had turned the lock when the sound of a servant coming into the room had driven her in a panic to relock the carved oaken door. All these years she had kept that tiny key in a little leather purse, and now the opportunity had passed.

A nobody! And Diana Martyn was right. A few months ago such a sneer would have provoked her laughter; but now – there was reason enough why the slur should be wiped out. She was sufficiently worldly-wise to foresee all the discreditable possibilities which might surround her birth. She knew of rich people who maintained children they might not own; and whilst there was no horror in the thought for her, there was a growing sense of dismay since Dick Hallowell had come into her life. She might tell him everything – everything she knew – and be certain of his sympathy and encouragement; she might even learn the worst and yet have no fear of his attitude and of losing his love.

She woke, thinking about Monk's Chase and the little cupboard, and in the afternoon she made her decision. Amongst her possessions was also the key of the postern door…

4

When Stimmings, the butler, bolted and chained the great door of Monk's Chase for the night, he reported to his uninterested master that it was "pouring heavens hard." It had been raining all the afternoon, and by dinner time the downpour was steady and voluminous. The rain pond began to form in the hollow beneath Lower Oaks; only the middle of the gravelled drive showed above the flanking torrents that ran down from Black Wood and the hill behind and formed a miniature lake about the lodge gates until the rim of it spread to the ditch.

A night as black as pitch and filled with the hissing of water; a night when cottagers sat beneath leaking roofs and planned new thatchings or cursed the parsimony of landlords.

The station fly from Worplethorpe came slowly through the downpour; the steady clop-clop of its ancient horse a melancholy accompaniment to groan and grind of steel-tyred wheels.

A tap on the window and the driver pulled at his wet reins, the door of the old landau screeched open and a slight figure stepped down into the road.

It was a girl, wrapped from chin to heel in a shining black oilskin. Her hat was pulled down almost over her eyes so that little of her face could be seen in the dim yellow light of the lamp.

"Thank you, this will do," she said. "I may be an hour – or less. Perhaps you can find some sort of shelter until I return."

The driver stooped over to speak and a rivulet of water poured from the curly brim of his hat.

"Didn't you want to go to the Chase, miss? I can take you up the drive to the house; you'll get wet through."

"No, thank you," she said hastily. "If you will wait here – I don't wish to – to wake the house."

She walked forward. The old horse did not so much as raise his drooping head as she passed in front of him.

The lodge was silent and deserted, the iron gates slightly ajar. In other days, she remembered, the old gardener lived here, but he had died when she was at school. Ankle deep, she splashed through the water, and was glad that in the one moment of sanity which had distinguished her plans, she had decided to bring her rubber boots. The crown of the drive was gained, but walking was no less uncomfortable, nor did the high poplars which bordered the straight drive afford her much protection.

The house would have been in sight, if anything was in sight, the moment she passed the lodge gates. She saw it presently, an undistinguishable mass against the hilly background. There were no lights. Evidently her information was accurate – Mr Hallett retired early. With a heart that was thumping painfully, she crossed the oval of lawn, a green island in a yellow sea (if it had been visible), and passed round the east wing.

She was mad – she told herself this every few seconds. Mad to go on, mad to think out this wild scheme, mad to go on with it; madder still now, as she stood with a key trembling in her hand before the little door in the grey, ivy-covered wall, to commit herself finally to this act of hers.

Yet, if all which had been told her was true, that behind the little door in the wall was the solution of all mysteries, then she was justified.

She put the key in the lock and turned it. At her push the door opened uneasily. From her pocket she took a little electric lamp, flashed it across the narrow stone passage before she closed the door and, moving silently in her rubber boots, climbed the three stone stairs to a second door. The key of the first opened this too. She was in a long, wide corridor, broadly carpeted. At intervals were little groups of statuary, old chairs and settees – the conventional decoration that was familiar to her.

Nothing had been disturbed since she was here last. The dull portraits in their heavy gold frames, the tapestry that covered a portion of the wall, the long crimson curtains at the end that hid the east window – she knew them so well!

Here the sound of the rain was hushed. She heard the big tick of the grandfather clock in the broad hall. Somewhere in the house the wind was rattling a loose window-sash. Drawing a deep breath, she went swiftly along the gallery, turned to the left and was in the hall. Again she stopped and listened, her eyes striving to pierce the darkness. A ghostly light showed the two long barred windows which flanked the main entrance. She could guess rather than see the curved stairway leading to the floor above. It required all her resolution to cross the hall and turn softly the handle of the library door.

A fire was burning; a big armchair obscured the grate, but she saw the red glow of it. Apparently the room was empty. She recognised the chair with an involuntary nod. It was that in which she used to curl herself when she was a long-legged schoolgirl, devouring the romances of Henty. And then she let her eyes travel around the room, and they stopped at the cupboard. She set her teeth, almost ran across the soft carpet, and with shaking fingers slipped in the tiny key she took from her bag…

Empty! Her mouth opened in amazement. The shallow hiding place held nothing…

Something made her look round, and she nearly dropped. From the chair was ascending a thin curl of blue smoke.

"Do you mind closing the door after you? It is rather draughty."

The voice was soft and muffled.

She stood staring in the direction of the voice, and then, in desperation, she whipped out a little Browning from her bag.

"Don't move!" she said in a low voice. "I – I am armed."

From the chair there rose a tall man, greyhaired, powerfully built, a pair of huge dark spectacles hiding his fine face. A big pipe dangled from his teeth. He wore evening dress, though his dinner jacket was of black velvet.

"Come and sit down – come nearer the fire," he said. "You must be wet."

She hesitated and then slowly came towards him, her shaking hand gripping the pistol.

"Don't move!" She hardly recognised her own voice. Then she heard his deep chuckle.

"I suppose you have a revolver or something equally dramatic in your hand? That's too bad!" And then: "I'm very serious about the door: do you mind closing it? I am rather susceptible to chills."

She went to the door. Here was her opportunity – should she fly? In a few seconds she would be outside the house. But he had seen her; it would be very undignified to leave that way. Queer how the question of dignity came to be considered at such a moment.

The door closed and she went back to the fire. He was sitting again, a pipe clenched between his teeth, his face turned to the glowing coals.

"You came in by the postern, I suppose? I must have the lock changed. Sit down, won't you?"

She hesitated.

"Oh, yes, I knew you were a woman," he went on, in his soft tone. "Guessed so when I heard the swish of your skirt, though of course it might have been a mackintosh. What do you want?"

She licked her lips; her throat was dry. She made two attempts before finally she articulated:

"I wanted something…that I thought was in this room. Nothing… valuable…to anybody but me. Can't you see…and guess?"

He smiled slowly.

"I can guess, but I cannot see. I am blind."

He made the announcement in such a matter-of-fact tone that she could not grasp its importance for a while.

"Blind?" she gasped. "Oh, I'm – I'm so sorry."

And yet her heart leapt. He could not see her – and would not recognise her again if he saw her.

"I really did not wish to rob you," she said. "Only – I – my people rented this place last summer – and – I left something behind which I did not wish anybody to know I had."

She was on safer ground here. She knew that in the summer months Monk's Chase had been let to a rich American family.

"Oh – you're one of the Osborn family, are you? Well, young lady, if you can find what you want, take it. I'm sorry I frightened you."

She looked round at the open cupboard door.

"It has been taken away," she said. "And now I'll go – may I?"

He rose and walked across the room, his fingers touching the furniture as he passed. Unerringly he turned to the right, traversed the hall and came to the little side passage. For a second he stood outside the postern door, the rain pelting down on him.

"Good night," he said. "I hope you will not get very wet."

He waited till the sound of her hurrying footsteps no longer came to him, then he turned back, locked and bolted the postern and returned to his study.

As he entered the room he switched on all the lights and made his way to the chair before the fire. For five minutes he sat motionless, his forehead wrinkled in a frown, then slowly he filled his pipe, lit it and, pushing up his dark spectacles, took up a newspaper from the chair and resumed the reading which the sound of the postern door opening had interrupted. And he read, without the aid of glasses, the very smallest type.

"Poor Hope Joyner!" he muttered between puffs of smoke. "Poor Hope Joyner!"

5

"I'm going to tell you the truth," said Hope Joyner desperately, and Dick Hallowell chuckled.

"A refreshing experience; I think I can endure it," he said. "What is worrying you, my dear?"

He took both her hands in his, and for a second they lay passive before she drew them away.

"You may not want to – know me after I've told you," she said jerkily. "Do you remember what that – what Diana Martyn said about me?"

"Diana says so many things about everybody that I can't keep track of them," said Dick, smiling.

"Of course you remember!" she scoffed. "She said I was 'a nobody.' "

"Which is absurd," said Dick, "for here you are, a very tangible and beautiful lady, giving me tea in your exquisite and expensive drawing-room; and you're just as substantial as the Ritz Hotel that I can see through your window."

"Don't be absurd," she said. "She meant I had no beginning, no origin, no parents...that there was a chance that I was – oh, anything horrible you can think of. You know something of heraldry; you realise what the bar sinister means."

"Oh, that!" said Dick. "But really, does it matter? Bar sinisters occur in all the best coats of arms – I am not so sure that it doesn't appear in mine!"

His ready acceptance of such a possibility took her breath away. For a moment she was relieved, in another instant irritated.

"I don't know that I am," she said. "It is horrid of you, Dick, to believe that I am!"

"I don't believe anything about you except that you're the dearest girl on God's earth, and I'm going to marry you, retire from the Army and live happy ever afterwards."

"Do be sensible, Dick – please! Don't you see what a horrible position I'm in? I don't know who sends me my money, I don't know anything about my parents, I'm just – nobody! I have to come back to that. Somehow it didn't matter, and I never worried, until – well, until you came into my life."

"And into the water," said the practical Dick, "I think I shall put a punt pole into my own quarterings – a punt pole *or* on a field *azur* – though the river is anything but *azur*."

She was thinking, her brow corrugated into tiny lines; then suddenly: "I'm going to tell you something," she said quietly, and without apologetic preamble, without explaining or excusing her act, she told him of her visit to Monk's Chase.

Dick listened seriously enough, and, when she had finished: "You were a little goop to take such a risk," he said. "Who is Hallett?"

She shook her head.

"I know nothing about him except that he's very rich and rather indifferent, so far as I am concerned. He has a big estate in Kent; in fact most of my childhood was spent there."

"You never saw him?"

She shook her head.

"Never. He travelled a great deal; in fact he was abroad all the time I was there. I asked his lawyers if he was any relation to me, and they were very emphatic on the point."

"He wasn't?" asked Dick.

"None whatever. He knew my mother – I have an idea there was some old romance, but of course I've never been able to discuss the subject with Mr Hallett. He is a trustee under my father's will – at least, I suppose he is."

"Have you ever seen the will?"

She shook her head.

"I've seen nothing, Dick. I only know that I receive an enormous allowance, and that when I meet the wrong kind of people – as once I did – I have a very sharp note from the lawyers telling me that I am making undesirable acquaintances. It is they who supply me with Carlow's List."

"And you have no other relations?"

"None," she replied, a little irritably, and then laughed. "You see, I am nobody!"

"I suppose you'll be getting a letter from your lawyers about me," he bantered. "If I am not undesirable myself, I have certainly undesirable relatives!"

He was thinking of his undesirable relatives as he walked down Piccadilly, and it was not so much a coincidence as it seemed that as he entered the Circus he came face to face with his brother. Graham Hallowell was no longer the shoddy, down-at-heel wastrel who had interviewed him at the Tower. He was the mirror of fashion, and from the tips of his enamelled shoes to the crown of his grey Homburg, an advertisement of efficient valeting. For a moment Dick was startled, then he smiled, and would have passed on had not Graham intercepted him.

"If you can sustain the disgrace of being seen with a jail-bird, I'd like to have a few words with you, Dick," he said coolly.

"Now is the time and the place," answered his brother; "but if it is money – "

Graham's lips curled in a sneer.

"Do you think of nothing but money?" he asked. "No, I want to talk to you about Diana."

The smile faded from Dick Hallowell's face.

"That is an even more profitless subject – " he began.

"She wants to be friends, that's all," said Graham roughly. "There's no sense in pursuing the vendetta. Can't you forget that she ever preferred somebody else to you?"

"If I remember it at all," said Dick quickly, "it is with a sense of gratitude – that is the one thing for which I thank her."

He looked at his watch.

"I'm afraid I can't give you any more time, Graham; I am meeting a friend in five minutes. But you may tell Diana from me that I harbour no resentment. Your talk of a vendetta is absurd. I only want not to meet her; not because she arouses any feeling of unhappiness in me, but because she stands for something that I loathe – treachery, duplicity, and it seems absurd to add to those mean qualities so mild a one as disloyalty."

With these words and a little nod he passed on, and Graham, standing on the sidewalk, watched him as he crossed the road and disappeared among the throng that was passing down Lower Regent Street.

Diana was waiting for him in her drawing-room, and with a woman's quick instinct she guessed that there had been a meeting between the brothers.

"He was his usual God Almighty self," growled Graham, as he dropped into an easy chair and searched his pockets for his cigarette case. "He has forgiven you but doesn't want any dealings with you."

"What did you expect?"

"I thought it would be easier if we got together again. But that fellow's like ferro-concrete."

She stood looking down at him, beating a slow, measured tattoo with her toe, her finger at her lips, her inscrutable eyes surveying him blankly.

"You are a fool," she said. "Did you speak to him about an allowance?"

Graham Hallowell laughed harshly.

"An allowance? What do you think Dick would have said to that? No, he squashed that idea before the conversation started. Besides, if Trayne really wants me for a job, there will be big money, and safety, too."

Diana bit her lip thoughtfully.

"What is the job?" she asked.

"How the devil do I know?" He was irritable. "Trayne doesn't tell you over the phone what he wants you for. I've never worked for him. You have, Diana?"

She evaded the question.

"He is very generous," she admitted – "and very dangerous."

"Why dangerous?" he was quick to ask.

"I think those kind of men must be," she said, still thoughtful. "The work he asked me to do wasn't very difficult, but I see now that it was necessary to his plan. It happened two years ago. I was asked to take Lord Firlingham to one of Trayne's gambling houses – a house he'd rented in Portland Place. I had to pretend I knew some people there, and we called in on our way back from the opera. Firlingham lost forty thousand pounds in one sitting at baccarat. I knew nothing about this for days after, for I left him there, and left him winning. The first intimation I had that they had made a 'killing' was when I received twenty hundred-pound bank-notes."

"Two thousand pounds!" He whistled. "That fellow certainly pays well."

"I hated the idea at first," she mused, "but Firlingham's a beast; one of the really unpleasant men I have met in town."

She looked at the little clock on the mantelpiece.

"We ought to be going."

Graham stared at her in surprise.

"Are you seeing Tiger, too?"

She nodded.

"I've had an intimation at third-hand from His Majesty that I might accompany you with profit to myself," she said dryly.

Not far from Soho Square are the handsome premises of the Mousetrap Club, a social institution which includes in its roll of membership some of the greatest names in the land. The luxury of its appointments no less than the unfashionable situation marked it as out of the ordinary. It was generally understood that here play was very high; but it was chiefly celebrated for its cuisine and the extraordinary moderation of its charges.

Despite the rumours of play, the place had never received the attention of the police. Once or twice, high officials from Scotland Yard mingled with the guests, but these had seen nothing more reprehensible than bridge at fifty pounds a hundred; and since the points at which bridge may be played is a purely domestic affair, and concerns only a club's committee, no action was called for. If baccarat was played, it was without the official knowledge of the club's management, and certainly no stranger was admitted to these séances unless he was well vouched for. Never once was there a suggestion that the game was anything but straight, and yet Mr Trayne, who both punted heavily and sometimes took the bank, inevitably rose a winner.

The luncheon crowd had cleared by the time Diana and her companion walked into the sedate vestibule.

"Mr Trayne is in the secretary's room," whispered the grey-haired hall porter, and the visitors followed him to the back of the premises, along a thickly carpeted corridor, until he came to a rosewood door and, stopping, knocked.

A voice bade them come in, and, turning the handle, the porter stood aside and let them pass into the room, closing the door behind them.

The man who raised his blue eyes in a passionless survey of the visitors was nearer to sixty than fifty. His close-cropped hair was grey, the clean-shaven, powerful face was almost unwrinkled. Even as he sat, his height was evident, the strength in the broad shoulders was impressive. The stub of a cigar was clenched between teeth of dazzling whiteness, too irregular to be any but those nature had given and careful attendance had preserved. This was Tiger Trayne, more lion than feline, more human at close quarters than Diana had expected.

He rose very slowly, took out his cigar and threw it into the fireplace.

"Welcome to our lair," he said, with a hint of humour in his eyes. "You are Diana Martyn, of course?"

He had a deep, rich voice; his speech was rather deliberate. Diana thought she had never met anybody in whom she was so agreeably disappointed. And she understood dimly why this mastermind in so many criminal enterprises had all his life escaped the processes of the law. She remembered all that Colley had told her – the traps that had been set for him, the elaborate system of entanglement which had been designed to his undoing. The best brains in two continents had schemed to net this tiger, but he had baffled them all.

"You ought to remember me, Mr Trayne," she said, and he showed his teeth in a smile.

"It is part of my policy to remember nobody, and to meet even my closest friends as strangers who need introducing all over again. It is a sound scheme – you should try it."

He was talking to her, but his eyes were on Graham.

"And you are Mr Hallowell of course! Sit down, won't you? Will you take coffee?"

He pressed a bell and, after a moment, gave the order, though no servant made an appearance and no telephone was visible. From the wall, apparently, a deep voice said "*Oui, m'sieur.*"

"It's my little loud speaker," he explained. "It is let in the panelling: you would not see it."

"Aren't you afraid of people listening to you?" asked Diana curiously, and he laughed.

"They can only listen when I wish. You have been in the country?"

He addressed Graham, who was well enough acquainted with the jargon of his late associates to understand the delicate reference to his imprisonment.

"Yes," he answered shortly.

"Unfortunate – very unfortunate." Tiger Trayne's voice was gently sympathetic. "You would not have gone into the country if you had had somebody to think for you. Generals are very poor hands with the bayonet, and the cleverest and bravest of fighting soldiers make indifferent generals."

He handed a box of cigars to the man, and as Graham selected one he went on:

"No man can be a successful criminal unless he has allied to him the police mind. Somebody who will think and reason as the detectives will reason. A burglar planning a coup, first of all makes himself blind to the perils of detection. When he has done that effectively, he goes ahead to create clues that even a short-sighted amateur could follow. Modern battles are won by rehearsal attacks over dummy positions."

They did not interrupt him, realising – at least, Diana realised at once – that this was not a garrulous man talking for the sake of talking, nor one anxious to air his knowledge and wisdom for their admiration, but that every word he said had an especial significance.

"Now if I were going to commit or to plan a big steal – here's the coffee."

The hidden lift made no sound that the visitors could hear, yet when he went to the wall and pulled aside a panel, there was the silver tray with its steaming cups waiting. He lifted it out, put it on the table, closed the panel with a touch of his hand, and waited for a while, his head bent, listening. Apparently satisfied, he dumped a large quantity of cream in his own cup, stirred it and drank it at a gulp.

"If I were planning a big coup, something that would bring the men and women who work the scheme, say – " he paused – "fifty thousand pounds, I should be very careful to rehearse the affair thoroughly. I would have the man practise climbing light ladders, dropping from a considerable height to his feet; I would have him study the drill book (if he had to deal with soldiers), and the orders and regulations of the place to which he would have to go; I would have him study the tides – "

"What is the job?" asked Graham impatiently.

The cold eyes were turned upon him.

"Did I speak of a job?" asked Tiger Trayne gently, almost reproachfully. "I am merely asserting a few principles."

A warning glance from Diana silenced the young man.

"I was sitting here this morning," Trayne went on, "dreaming. I don't know what started it: I think it must have been the account of the trial at the Old Bailey yesterday. The crude minds of the criminal classes! Here is a man sent to penal servitude for a clumsy burglary which yielded him less than a hundred pounds. How absurd, thought I. He might have taken less risks, and displayed the same resolution, and there were fifty thousand pounds for him and no come back. Fifty thousand pounds!" he mused. "That's a lot of money!"

He paused, as though inviting comment, but, warned by Diana, Graham Hallowell was silent.

"There is no glory in a common burglary," said Trayne, looking absently through the window upon Soho Square. "And believe me, glory counts, if a man has imagination. If I were a burglar I should like to see the record of my crime with staring headlines in the newspapers; I would like to do something so sensational that all the world would be talking about me."

Again he stopped, pursed his lips, brought his eyes slowly first to Diana's, then to Graham's face.

"It is three hundred years since a bungler attempted one of the most remarkable steals of all time. He was a swashbuckling, drunken lout of a man, and nearly got away with it, without aeroplanes or motorboats or any of the assistance which modern science gives to a man nowadays. This Colonel Blood – "

Despite herself, Diana gave a little cry, but apparently the name had no significance to Graham Hallowell.

"This Colonel Blood made a miserable failure of his attempt – and deserved to. Was he hanged? I forget. Does one get hanged for stealing the Crown jewels – "

Graham Hallowell was on his feet, his mouth opened in horror and amazement.

"The – the Crown jewels?" he gasped.

"Their value – let us say a million sterling." Tiger Trayne was oblivious to the interruption. "The sentimental value, infinitely more. A mad idea, you will say? I thought so when I first had it broached to me – it was certainly a madman's idea. For what satisfaction could any man have out of fitting to his ill-shaped head the Crown of England – not for the admiration of his ragged subjects, but secretly, in some dark, hot room in Kishlastan to which even his harem was not admitted?"

Even Diana was guilty of an indiscretion. "You mean the Prince of Kish – " He silenced her with a gesture.

"I know of no princes. India is a country which has no appeal for me. I am merely putting into words the fragments of idle dreams. A madman's idea...yet madmen are akin to genius, and very brilliant schemes are hatched in these addled brains at times. Especially if they are obsessed. An obsession takes peculiar forms. Some men dream of women, some of power. I knew a man who thought of nothing day and night but the game of cribbage, and another who collected china and who would weep at the breaking of a plate. Others are crazy on the subject of jewellery, of precious stones – " He sighed. "The human mind can never be generalised; it has such queer expressions." And then, at a tangent: "Fifty thousand pounds is a mint of money. And all for a few weeks' rehearsal, the careful adherence to instructions... practically no risk – a broken head or two, but not yours, supposing," he added apologetically, "that anything so unthinkable should happen as your taking part in such an adventure."

Graham Hallowell was white and shaking. He cleared his throat, in spite of which his voice was husky.

"Does anything more direct and explicit follow on this?" he asked.

Tiger Trayne rose and went to a safe in the wall, unlocked it with a key that was attached to a chain in his pocket, and took out a brown paper-covered volume, the size of a thick exercise book. He turned the leaves rapidly and Graham saw that they were typewritten.

"Here is my little romance, one of the very few I have written," said Mr Trayne as he lit a cigar slowly, keeping his elbow on the book. "I have taken a leaf from another author's composition, and I have sited my story in a Ruritania of my own. In this Ruritania there is a castle called Strong. It stands on the banks of a wide river, and is a thousand years old. In this castle is a tower, strongly guarded, which contains the jewels of the reigning Prince. In my idle moments I have worked out a scheme whereby a resolute and clever man, acting rigidly under instructions, succeeds in abstracting those jewels. It is an ingenious tale. I have made the book so that it will fit a man's pocket, and if you read my poor effort you will find that I have called the jewels 'fruit,' the guard the 'watchman.' If by chance the book fell into other hands, it might be difficult for an unauthorised and uninstructed person to understand. The question is" – he spun the edges of the leaves carelessly – "are you interested enough to devote your mind to the study of this interesting romance?"

Graham nodded.

"There is a small furnished cottage advertised in this morning's newspapers," said Mr Trayne. "You will find it in the third column of page nine of the *Megaphone*. If you applied to rent the cottage for a month or two, I think the agents would let you have it at a reasonable price. A caretaker has been left in charge, and I have no doubt that if you asked him civilly, or even if you didn't ask him at all, you would find this book on your table every night at eight o'clock. It would be taken away at two o'clock in the morning; but in less than a month you should memorise every word."

He took out a pocketbook, extracted a newspaper cutting and handed it to Graham.

"Here is the advertisement."

"I'll write today," said Graham huskily.

Mr Trayne nodded, replaced the book in the safe, and, rising, stretched himself, his amused eyes on Diana.

"I have another little romance for you to read, Miss Martyn," he said, "but I will talk to you about that later."

He walked to the window and stared out, his hands deep in his pockets. Looking past him, Diana saw a familiar figure and gasped.

"How queer!" she said.

"What is queer?" Tiger Trayne did not look round.

"Why that is the wretched woman who came to my flat this morning to ask me if I wanted a maid! The creature actually walked into the hall; I found her outside the door of my drawing room."

"Really?" Mr Trayne did not turn his head. "How fascinating! You mean the fat woman – let me see, what does she call herself?"

"Mrs Ollorby," said Diana.

Trayne nodded gravely.

"She told you her real name," he said. "That is Jane Ollorby."

"Do you know her?" she said in surprise.

"Yes, I know her," said Tiger Trayne slowly. "She is one of the cleverest women detectives on the books of Scotland Yard. I hope, before you found her outside your drawing room door, that you were not discussing anything of vital importance."

Diana felt the colour leaving her cheeks. "But – what – did she want to find out? Why is she here? Has she followed me?"

She was a little incoherent.

"It is very probable. Idle curiosity is a very forgivable quality in a woman, but Mrs Ollorby's curiosity rather goes beyond idleness."

He turned upon her a smiling face.

"A detective watches, not necessarily because he or she knows, but because he wants to know. I've been watched so consistently throughout my life that I should feel uncomfortable if I wasn't! She probably wishes to know why Mr Graham Hallowell is calling upon you, or, if she knows the reason, what are his plans for the future. Scotland Yard takes a great interest in people who are released from penal servitude."

"Watching me, is she?" said Graham savagely. "I'll stop that – "

"You'll stop nothing." Mr Trayne's voice was very gentle but very firm. "Let her watch – it is good for her eyes."

"She looks more like a washerwoman," said Diana in wonder.

"She has washed a great deal of dirty linen, most of it in public," said Trayne ironically. "And she's a very thorough laundress, believe me! Perhaps" – he hesitated – "perhaps it would be better, Miss Martyn, if you took the cottage at Cobham and invited friend Hallowell down. That is, if you can survive such an outrage on the proprieties? I think you can because" – he knit his brow – "I can't remember exactly how long you have been married to our friend Graham, but I have an idea it was a month before he went to prison."

Diana's lips tightened, but she said nothing. So that little secret was not wholly hers!

"At a Worcestershire register office, was it not?" asked Trayne, with the air of a man who was striving to recall something that had escaped his memory. "And in the name – but does that matter?"

"I don't think it does," said Diana coolly. "You have a very good information bureau, Mr Trayne."

He smiled.

"It is rather – adequate," he said. "You and your husband might care to study the little book together."

"Suppose I don't want to come into this?" asked Diana. "Does that make a difference?"

Trayne shrugged his broad shoulders.

"The difference between fifty thousand and a hundred thousand," he said, "and possibly more to follow. Conceive, if you can, my dear Miss Martyn, the huhlaballoo that would rise throughout the world. Do you remember the disappearance of Da Vinci's Mona Lisa? Intensify that a hundredfold. The fruit – let us call it – has gone. Payment has been made by the gentleman on whose behalf it was taken. What sum do you think the owners of the fruit would pay to get it back – and no questions asked? And no prosecution if the truth came out."

"You mean you'd double-cross – " began Graham.

" 'Double-cross' is Greek to me," said Mr Trayne suavely. "I find it difficult to keep myself *au courant* with modern thieves' slang, and especially modern American thieves' slang."

He examined the long ash of his cigar intently.

"And now I think you had better go," he said. "I am rather curious to see what Mrs Ollorby does – I rather think that with your retirement the Mousetrap Club will no longer be honoured by her embarrassing observation."

As they were going: "By the way," said Trayne, "Mr Colley Warrington is not in my confidence. I tell you this in case, in an unguarded moment, you should imagine he was."

He had emphasised "my," and as they drove homeward Diana wondered in whose confidence Mr Warrington might be. Graham had other thoughts. From time to time he glanced back through the window at the back of the car for a glimpse of Mrs Jane Ollorby, who had watched their departure from the Mousetrap Club with such unfeigned interest.

6

His Excellency the Prince of Kishlastan sat cross-legged on a divan in his private room, his dark eyes staring into vacancy, his thin brown hands playing with a chain of emeralds that hung from his neck. From time to time he took from his pocket a small golden box, dipped his finger into the yellowish powder with which it was half filled, and touched finger to tongue before he snapped the box and put it away in the voluminous folds of his silken gown.

By his side was a pad of press cuttings, and after a while, and with every evidence of disgust, he took up the packet and read one after the other of the printed slips.

Rikisivi, Prince of Kishlastan, had been educated in England at a great public school. His knowledge of English was perfect. Nevertheless, such was his antipathy to his overlords that he maintained the farce of conducting all his official conversations through an interpreter. His antipathy was a real one. He was the son of a hundred kings who had lorded it in the old days before the John Company had come to India, had given the law of life and death and had ruled, sometimes wisely, more often brutally, a debased population that had worshipped the members of his house as so many divinities. There was talk of deposition in the air, the putting down of one ruler and the exaltation of another. He might be asked to retire to Paris, the recipient of a government pension, whilst his successor handled the enormous riches that had accumulated through a thousand years.

The offence that had brought him before the Governor of Pondicherry need not be described. There was murder in it, cold-blooded assassination, the torture of one woman, the disappearance of another. The beautiful Eurasian who had vanished amidst the colonnades of his palace had almost brought him to ruin. Had she been found and questioned, the ruin would have been absolute; but she was never found, and never would be found, till the earth yielded up its dead and a certain lovely garden was disturbed by the spades of searchers.

The memory of his success in baffling these shrewd political officers and their bloodhounds always brought a sense of exhilaration to him. He tasted the illusive fruits of infallibility. What had been done once might be done again, and no one be the wiser; but, he thought, as his dark eyes stared unwinkingly into space, it was one thing to bring a half-willing girl secretly from the bazaars of Kishlastan, to the purlieus of his white palace, and another matter to transport over thousands of miles of sea and land the wholly unwilling victim of his caprice. Once in Kishlastan, no eye would see, no ear would hear, no tongue would tell; for his people offered him a fanatical devotion. It would be a wonderful vengeance on these men who had slighted him, who had covertly threatened his very princeship…

But how might it be accomplished? He had thought of a dozen, a hundred ways, and rejected them all.

Behind the curtained door he heard a soft knock and rang his bell as a signal that the caller could enter. It was his interpreter, who spoke in a low tone to his master.

"Let him come in," nodded the Prince, and Colley Warrington was ceremoniously bowed into the quiet apartment.

Did he bring a solution? Rikisivi watched him through half-closed eyes and wondered.

Mr Warrington was one of the favoured few who could obtain an audience at any hour. He had been very useful to the Indian in very curious ways; so curious, indeed, that it had required no effort on the part of Rikisivi to broach the subject that was uppermost in his mind. But they talked of many things before they came to the vital matter of Hope Joyner.

"This side would be easy," said Colley confidently. "Whether it would be possible to get her through India to Kishlastan, you know better than I. I don't even know the nature of the shore – whether it is possible to land on any unfrequented part of the coast – "

The rajah nodded.

"That would be simple," he said; "much easier than here in England. A woman travels *purdah* – that is behind closed curtains, and it would be as much as an official's job was worth to attempt to search a car. But here – " He shook his head.

"It will be dangerous," said Colley, "but not impossible. In fact, rajah, it would be a question of money. How do you travel back to the East?"

"By P & O," said the Prince, and Colley rubbed his chin.

"It would mean the chartering of a yacht," he said, "and even that would be risky – you'd be at the mercy of the crew – but it could be done."

He named a sum – a fortune – but Riki dismissed the question of cost with an impatient gesture.

"Money is – nothing. You would require help. This man Trayne – "

"Not Trayne," said Colley decisively. "I know that you have some sort of dealings with him, and I am not curious to know what it is. Trayne would turn it down anyway. He is rather squeamish about women."

He related a story that had come to him of Trayne's "squeamishness" – a story almost entirely creditable to the Tiger; would have been wholly so, but mixed up in it was a thread of something like piracy on the high seas, for Mr Trayne had many interests and his activities covered half the world.

"No, I don't know her," he said, answering an inquiry. "Some friends of mine do. She's pretty... I suppose she would not go willingly?"

The Indian stared at him.

"Am I such a fool as to ask her?" he demanded. "No. I shall not see her again. I have written apologising for my blunder about the pearls; that is the end of our acquaintance. Miss Martyn knows the girl. She would help you?"

Colley hesitated.

He had no illusions about the foulness of the act he was contemplating so coolly. A lifetime spent in the slimes had destroyed whatever there was in his nature which might have received the Prince's proposal with loathing. He had trafficked all his life in delicate commodities. Honour, that imponderable substance which is called "self-respect," decency – all the big, clean things of life were phenomena to be observed and exploited in other men and women. He had his own sense of values and was not without his own ideals. The grossest of men, without the disposal of one artistic faculty, may admire the beauty of a Corot without desiring either to paint or yet to dwell amidst the sylvan loveliness his genius translated to canvas. He could admire beauty and innocence as a butcher might admire the lamb his knife will slaughter. An abstract admiration; not to interfere with business. It was Colley's boast that he owed no man a penny, and had never kept a woman waiting a second when he made an appointment. His very perversion demanded that he should possess minor excellences.

He drove to Diana's flat and arrived in time to see her disappear through the doorway of the building followed by Graham. And he found the two strangely silent and preoccupied.

"Well – what did Trayne want?" he asked, almost as he entered the room.

"Nothing much." Diana turned the subject.

"Curious devil – old Trayne. The super-Fagin. They say he speaks every European language except Hungarian! By the way, Diana, have you seen little Joyner lately?"

Diana looked at him suspiciously.

"By 'little Joyner' you mean the mysterious young person of Devonshire House? No; we are not on calling terms. Why?"

He could shrug off the question.

"I thought I saw her as I drove here," he said, and asked again: "What did Trayne want?"

Diana was the readier liar.

"He is starting a new gambling house off Portland Square," she said glibly, "but I told him that had no appeal for me."

His keen eyes were watching her, and she guessed his scepticism before he spoke.

"That is not like Trayne. He doesn't as a rule consult outsiders before he starts something," he said.

"Perhaps he wanted to discuss Hope Joyner," said Diana tartly.

It was a shot at a venture, but she saw his expression change.

"Did he?" he asked quickly. "What did he want to know about her?"

He almost betrayed himself in that moment of surprise, but, recovering quickly as he read her face, he laughed.

"I shouldn't be surprised at anything Tiger did," he said, with an assumption of carelessness which deceived nobody. "And did his offer – I suppose he made an offer – extend to Graham?"

There was a hint of a sneer in his voice. He had never concealed his dislike for Graham, and the woman often wondered whether Colley Warrington knew the "secret" that was at least no secret to Tiger Trayne.

"I don't suppose Tiger will thank you for nosing into his mysteries," Colley went on. "He is a queer devil, as I've said before, and the less one has to do with him, the better for one's peace of mind."

He turned the conversation to another channel, and presently Diana asked a surprising question. For once Colley was without information.

"Mrs Ollorby?" he said. "No, I don't know that I've heard of the lady. Is she in our orbit?"

He was evidently ignorant of the woman's identity, and Diana thought it wise not to pursue the inquiry.

Mrs Ollorby was to become something of an irritation with Diana, a figure that hovered in the background of her thoughts – an irritation because of her very unimportance. If the woman was watching, it was Tiger Trayne who was the object of her curiosity. The true explanation of her unease might be found in the fact that never before had Diana found herself even remotely associated with the police. Was she now to have this experience? Not a pleasant thought this.

As the hours passed, the enormity of Trayne's plan slowly dawned upon her. She passed a sleepless night, tossing from side to side in her bed, and before dawn came she was half resolved to go no further in the matter, a resolve which she communicated to Graham when he came round to see her soon after breakfast.

He laughed scornfully.

"There is no danger in it, if Trayne is behind the scheme," he said. "Fifty thousand pounds may seem nothing to you, with a rajah's fortune to draw upon, but it means a whole lot to me. I'm tired of the dog's life I'm living."

"Mrs Ollorby – " she began.

"Mrs Fiddlesticks!" he scoffed. "What has she to do with us? She's watching the Mousetrap Club."

Diana shook her head.

"Why did she come to the flat?" she demanded. "Why did she stand outside my door listening? I'm perfectly sure Dombret told the truth when she said that she had shut the front door – this woman must have had a key of her own. I'm scared, Graham, and so would you be, if you gave the matter a little more thought."

He bit his lip and frowned.

"We ought to have told Trayne about the woman," he said. "If I can see him this morning, I'll ask him what he thinks about it."

When he rang up the Mousetrap, Mr Trayne was not there – or at least that was the message which came back to him. The grey-haired porter (he recognised his voice) suggested that Mr Trayne might possibly be taking an *apéritif* at the Brasserie Royale, and, accepting this hint, Graham strolled off to Piccadilly and had hardly taken his seat in the long room at one of the marble-topped tables, when he saw Trayne enter, a cigar between his teeth. After a casual glance round, he made his leisurely way to where Hallowell was sitting. Graham spoke to him again of what had happened on the previous day, and to his surprise the Tiger took a more serious view of the happening than he had taken previously.

"What was Miss Martyn talking about?"

"I forget for the moment," said Graham. "Of course, it may have been an accident that she got into the flat at all – "

Trayne shook his head.

"Mrs Ollorby doesn't have those kinds of accidents!" he said. "I take off my hat to that female! If it was an accident, why did she pretend she wanted a job? No, sir, there was no accident in that. She came by design, opened the door, because she suspected something. Now what on earth could she suspect, unless she knew I had asked to see Miss Martyn?"

He pulled at his lip thoughtfully.

"Possibly it was not your lady but you she was 'nosing,' " he said. "It is rather alarming."

"Does it alarm you?" asked Graham.

A slow smile dawned on the handsome old face.

"Not me," he said almost cheerfully. "I happen to know Ollorby's position at Scotland Yard."

He explained that the stout lady had once been a policeman, and owed her promotion to an official position at police headquarters to her extraordinary memory of faces; for having seen a portrait of Bert Howle, a forger for whose body the police of Europe were searching, she had not only recognised but had brought about his arrest, and, with the assistance of a policeman, had had him taken to the police station.

"She holds a sort of roving commission; in fact she's a sort of crime-finder," explained Tiger. "I've never heard of her being put on any particular job, her business being to make work for the male sleuths. And she has been lucky!"

He enumerated a number of cases that the woman had unearthed, and Graham was surprised by their magnitude and importance.

"She is Scotland Yard's official freelance," Tiger went on, "but you need never worry about her paying you attention – the fact that she's watching doesn't mean she suspects you of any offence, but that she's hoping to suspect you!"

He made no further reference to Mrs Ollorby.

Graham expected further details about the great plan, and it seemed that the conversation would be taken up where it had been put down the previous day, when Tiger Trayne asked him if he had written to the house agent. But apparently his employer had no intention of discussing the subject any further, for he went off at a tangent to talk about a mutual acquaintance, and it was not until Graham had paid the score and Trayne had risen to go that he returned to the Tower adventure, and then in so indirect and obscure a fashion that not until he had gone did the younger man realise that what he said was remotely connected with the scheme.

"I suppose you're not interested in shipping?" he asked apropos of nothing.

Graham shook his head.

"Have you by any chance seen or heard of the *Pretty Anne*?"

"No," replied Graham, in surprise. "What is she, a fishing boat?"

"She is not a fishing boat."

Trayne was very deliberate; it was almost as though he were delivering a legal judgment, he seemed to pick and choose his words with such care.

"The *Pretty Anne* is a seagoing ship, not large and not, I imagine, classed A1 at Lloyd's. If I were you, I should learn something about the *Pretty Anne* and scrape acquaintance with her skipper and owner." He paused. "His name is Eli Boss, and he is not – what shall I say? – a University man! You will not meet him at the Master Mariners' Club – I believe his favourite house of call is the 'Three Jolly Sailors' in Limehouse."

Graham listened in astonishment.

"Do you want me to see him?" he asked, and Mr Trayne smiled.

"I want you to do whatever you wish to do: I really don't insist that you take the cottage in the country, but if you took it, it would be pleasing to me. I make no request that you should get acquainted with Captain Eli Boss, but if by chance you found yourself on talking terms I should be pleased." And then: "Do you mind waiting fully five minutes after I have gone? I do not think it is advisable that we should be seen on the street together."

Graham suddenly remembered a question he had intended asking.

"We get a certain sum if we succeed, Mr Trayne," he said lowering his voice. "What happens if, through no fault of ours, we fail?"

Again that wry smile.

"You cannot fail," was the simple answer. "There is a mind behind this little adventure."

7

Hope Joyner had a very light postbag, and though the inevitable circulars and trade advertisements came in normal volume, her own private correspondence was small.

That morning, when her maid brought her letters in with the tea, she saw a familiar blue envelope, and with a little grimace extracted it from the other letters. Her lawyer seldom wrote, but when he did, there was something unpleasant to be said, and this missive was no exception.

> DEAR MISS JOYNER, *the letter ran,* We have learnt that you are acquainted with a Mr Hallowell. We feel that your trustees would not approve of this acquaintance, and it is our duty to inform you that Hallowell, although an educated man, has served a term of imprisonment for fraudulent conversion. In the circumstances it might be advisable to discontinue an acquaintance which must necessarily be an unprofitable and possibly a painful one.
>
> We are, dear Miss Joyner,
>
> Yours faithfully,

She looked down at the letter, her forehead puckered, and then smiled slowly, for she saw what had happened. The benevolent spy who overlooked her movements had made the mistake of confounding Dick Hallowell with his brother. She should have been very much annoyed, but the error was so palpable that she could afford to laugh.

Poor Dick! That was the most unkindest cut of all, to mistake him for his wretched brother. Her first inclination was to write back, pointing out the mistake. But a spirit of mischief restrained her. Perhaps she would receive a number of these epistles, growing in vehemence. It would be rather amusing to collect them for Dick's benefit, and eventually stagger the writer with the proof of their mistake.

The maid had set her bath ready and now was laying out her clothes.

"A woman called to see you this morning, miss. I didn't much like the look of her, so I told her you were out – she looked as though she wanted a job."

Hope shook her head.

"I'd rather you didn't send people away until I know who they are and what they want," she said, not for the first time in similar circumstances.

"I'm very sorry, miss." Janet was conventionally apologetic. "But I only did it because I thought – "

Janet was a little officious, though otherwise a good maid, and of late Hope had the faintest of suspicions that her lawyers, who gained such mysterious information about her movements and her acquaintances, might perhaps be indebted to the girl for their knowledge.

She had nearly finished her dressing and had slipped into her dress when Janet came in with the announcement that the caller had returned.

"A Mrs Johnson, miss," she said, as though eager to repair her earlier fault – as fault it was, if her mistress' manner meant anything. "She's called about the Young Women of India Committee."

This did not make "Mrs Johnson" any more welcome, for Hope had decided that this branch of philanthropy was not her forte, and had already written a letter of resignation. She hesitated.

"I'll see her in a moment," she said, and a few minutes later she went into her beautiful little drawing-room to find a large, broad-shouldered woman with a masculine face gazing pensively down upon Piccadilly. Hope's look of inquiry was met by an expansive and disarming smile.

"I'm sorry to disturb you so early, Miss Joyner," said the visitor, "and I think I'll save myself a lot of lying by telling you that I'm not from the Young Women of India Committee at all, and that my name is Ollorby."

It meant nothing to Hope, but her next words were rather alarming.

"I'd rather nobody knew I'd called," she went on. "The fact is, Miss Joyner, I am from police headquarters."

She produced a card with lightning dexterity which would not have been discreditable in a conjurer, and Hope Joyner read: "Mrs Emily Ollorby, Room 385, New Scotland Yard."

She looked at the visitor in surprise.

"A detective?" she said, and Mrs Ollorby's smile grew even broader.

"I'd like to call myself that, Miss Joyner," she said genially. "We fat women have our romantic moments. But I'm just Mrs Ollorby, who spends her life putting her ugly nose into other people's business. The Lord made some of us beautiful and some of us useful – every time I look at myself in a mirror I realise how useful I've got to be! Poor Ollorby, he was a hero! That man had his faults, but he certainly had courage. Maybe he had a sense of humour too, though I never discovered it, and the only funny thing he ever did was to marry me!"

She had a booming, chuckling voice, and Hope found herself smiling as Mrs Ollorby rattled on in her inconsequent way.

"It's funny how the criminal mind works," she continued. "I have never got a bad man into serious trouble but he didn't throw my looks in my face – and that's the proper place for 'em! I've been compared with everything in the farmyard, except the chicken – and maybe the duck. But I'm not sensitive. If I were, I should be dead. I've had men at the Old Bailey who've said they'd rather have another ten years added to their sentence than marry me, but I guess that's only their persiflage."

She paused to take breath, her bright eyes surveying the girl good-humouredly.

"And now you're wondering why I've come into your beautiful little flat. It wasn't to speak about myself, Miss Joyner, but about you. You're a member of the Young Women of India Committee, aren't you?"

Hope shook her head.

"I was, but I've resigned."

"Oh!" Mrs Ollorby, who knew so many things, evidently was unacquainted with this development. "That's that," she said. "It is evident you don't want me to tell you anything about that fake. Is Mr Hallett a personal friend of yours?"

The unexpectedness of the question momentarily silenced the girl.

"I've only met him once," she answered, and then, with a smile: "Is *he* a desperate criminal?"

Mrs Ollorby shook her head.

"Nothing desperate about Hallett," she said, "as far as I can discover. He's blind, too, and blind criminals are rare. No, I'm sort of interested in him. But then, I'm interested in so many people. Take the Prince of Kishlastan: he's a nice-looking fellow."

"I think he's hideous," said Hope, and Mrs Ollorby grinned again.

"Miss Diana Martyn – is she a friend of yours?"

"No," said Hope shortly.

"H'm!" Mrs Ollorby fingered one of her many chins. "Graham Hallowell, of course, you wouldn't know. You're acquainted with his brother, though? Nice-looking fellow. I saw him in the Tower the other day. Let me think…" She screwed her face into a terrific frown. "Didn't I see you there with him?"

"You may have done," said Hope, a little coldly.

"The Tower gets me all swimmy," said Mrs Ollorby. "Frozen history! Do you go there very often, Miss Joyner?"

Hope motioned her to a chair, and when the woman was seated, she sat down herself.

"Now, please, don't be mysterious. What have you come to ask me?" she said quietly. "If it is anything I can tell you, of course I will. But obscure people rather worry me."

"They worry me too," said Mrs Ollorby, in no sense abashed. "I'll tell you why I've come, Miss Joyner." She opened a huge leather bag which had been under her arms and had the appearance of being a portfolio, and after a search she took out a small sheet of paper, on which somebody had scribbled notes.

"I'm going to ask you a plain question, and I dare say you'll think it is impertinent and if you ring your bell and order that little bit of fluff to turn me out, I'm not going to be surprised."

This reference to Janet, who was certainly on the fluffy side of humanity, forced a smile from Hope, but she was too curious to be diverted.

"You're a friend of Sir Richard Hallowell, of the Berwick Guards, and now I'm going to ask you plainly the question that is in my mind. Are you engaged to Sir Richard?"

"No," said Hope.

"Is he a very dear friend of yours?"

The girl hesitated.

"Yes," she said at last, "he is a very dear friend of mine."

"Is he such a dear friend" – Mrs Ollorby spoke very slowly – "that he would do anything in the world for you?"

Hope stared at the woman.

"I don't understand – " she began.

"Are you lovers?" asked Mrs Ollorby bluntly, and the flush that came to the girl's face was her answer.

Before Hope could master her voice the older woman went on quickly: "You'll think I have a nerve, and so I have! But what I want to tell you is this, young lady, that Sir Richard Hallowell is by my standard a good man, and I want you to hesitate well before you ask him to do anything that a good man should not do."

Hope could only shake her head helplessly. "I haven't the slightest idea what you're driving at, Mrs Ollorby," she said; "but you may be sure that I should never ask Richard to do anything dishonourable, and I'm rather annoyed that you should suggest I would."

"I'm not suggesting you would." Mrs Ollorby was very emphatic. "I'm only wondering whether" – she hesitated – "maybe I've made a mess of it. I've certainly given you reason to be angry, even if you're not. Have you ever asked Richard Hallowell to do you a favour – a favour which would mean a neglect of duty on his part?"

"Of course I haven't!" said Hope indignantly. "Really, Mrs Ollorby, you're something more than mysterious."

"Aren't I?" Mrs Ollorby was penitence itself. "Not more, but worse! You see, Miss Joyner, I'm in a very delicate position. I know a lot of things that I ought not to know – if you were as wise as I am, there wouldn't be any need to beat about the bush." She sighed heavily. "But you're not! You don't know Tiger Trayne, of course? You wouldn't: he doesn't move in your set. And Mr Graham Hallowell – you don't know him?" She paused.

"I know of him," said Hope quietly. "He is Sir Richard's brother, and he has been – in trouble. The truth is that Richard and he are not good friends, and of course I've never been introduced to him, though – "

She stopped and smiled, as she remembered the letter of that morning.

"Though some people think you have?" suggested Mrs Ollorby shrewdly.

She closed her bag with a snap.

"Sir Richard Hallowell is a nice man," she said. "I don't know anybody I admire more, unless it is you! That's barefaced flattery, but frankness is my weakness."

She held the visiting card that Hope had handed back to her, and now, turning it over, she wrote rapidly with a pencil which she produced from some hidden pocket, and put the card into the girl's hand.

"That's my private address. I may not be there for a few days, but if you're in any kind of trouble, or you're worried about anything that you do not wish to bother Sir Richard with, maybe you'll phone me?"

"What sort of trouble am I likely to have?" asked the girl, half amused and half irritated.

Mrs Ollorby shrugged her broad shoulders.

"God knows," she said piously. "London is the kind of city where trouble comes easier than measles in a crèche." She walked briskly to the door. "I'd be glad if you would do me one favour, Miss Joyner. Do you mind not telling that little maid of yours my name and occupation?"

Before Hope could answer tartly that she was not in the habit of taking her maid into her confidence, Mrs Ollorby was gone.

The stout woman walked quickly down Piccadilly towards the Circus, humming a tune in a deep bass undertone, and seemingly oblivious of the world and its inhabitants. Behind her, at a distance, stalked a lank, thin, red-haired youth who wore a pair of terrifying horn-rimmed spectacles. His coat was a little too small for him, the sleeves and trousers so short that he displayed generous expanses of wrist and ankle. He never lost sight of Mrs Ollorby, but followed her into the tube station and was in the same elevator that brought her to the surface at Tottenham Court Road. Into Charlotte Street turned the stout lady and her trailer, and when Mrs Ollorby passed through an uninviting door, the young man stopped, waited for a few minutes with his back to the railings, staring up and down the street, and then followed her, taking from his pocket a large key, and pausing on the doorstep to blow the dust from the depression at its end.

Without knocking, he opened the door of a small parlour. Mrs Ollorby was taking off her beaded bonnet and hardly turned her head at his entrance. The young man sat down on a horsehair sofa and waited her pleasure.

"Well, Hector?" she asked.

"A feller followed you as far as the tube station at Tottenham Court Road, but he didn't come any farther," said Hector in a cracked voice.

"What sort of a feller?" asked his mother, for she bore that relationship to the lank youth.

"Well, ma" – Hector scratched his frosty nose – "he looked like a foreign feller. He was waiting outside the flats when you came out. I kept behind him, so I knew he was trailing you. It's a funny thing about me" – Hector rubbed his red hair complacently – "that whilst I see them, they don't spot me."

Mrs Ollorby smiled broadly.

"Nothing's more certain in the world, Hector, than that he spotted you!" she said good-temperedly. "You're like a red-headed lighthouse, Hector: they couldn't miss you. But it cramps their style to know they're being trailed too, Hector. That's why you're useful."

He glared at her ruefully.

"I don't see that I'm much use, ma," he said, in a despondent tone. And then, hopefully: "I suppose if I dyed my hair – "

"You'd look awful," said Mrs Ollorby, and then, as she patted him on the shoulder: "Don't worry, Hector; you're going to be a detective one of these days. I was speaking to the Commissioner about you this morning. They'll never let you into the force because of your eyesight, but I'll get a job for you, and you'll see your name in the paper, believe me."

He cheered visibly at this, for Mr Hector Ollorby's supreme ambition was to follow in his father's footsteps. The late Mr Ollorby had been a police-sergeant with a distinguished record, a fact which had made his wife's entry to the force during the war a fairly easy one.

There was a telephone instrument in the room and she called a Treasury number, dismissing with a jerk of her head her obedient progeny. For fully ten minutes she talked, whilst Hector stood in the passage, his hands to his ears, on guard. After a while his mother came out, and, pausing on the stairs to give instructions to the little maid-of-all-work, went up to her room and to bed. She had been up late on the previous night, but it seemed that there was a possibility of a sleepless night to follow.

Dusk had fallen on Charlotte Street when she came down. She had changed her clothes and the change was decidedly for the worse. She had the appearance of a woman who was in the last throes of respectable poverty. Her clothes were old, if tidy; her dingy bonnet, her down-at-heel shoes, had a pathetic aspect of hopeless struggle against circumstances.

She waited till night fell before she sallied forth, carrying a worn canvas handbag, and ten o'clock was striking when she arrived at a mean street in the East End of London, and, threading her way through the regiment of squawking children that littered the sidewalk, paused before No. 27 and knocked.

The slatternly woman who opened the door brought with her the aroma of stale spirits. She peered short-sightedly at the visitor half revealed in the naked light of a tiny oil lamp.

"Hallo!" she said ungraciously. "You've come, have you – I'd give you up."

"I don't see why you should give me up when I've paid my rent in advance," said Mrs Ollorby blandly.

The landlady muttered something under her breath and led the way up the uncarpeted stairs, pushed open the door of a small room, and revealed a bed, none too clean, which, with a small washstand and a chair, comprised the furniture of the apartment.

"I don't let lodgin's to wimmin as a rule," she said, "but you bein' out all day makes a difference."

She was slipshod of speech, after the manner of her kind, and was merely indicating that the acceptance of her new lodger was based upon Mrs Ollorby's statement that she would not occupy the room between nine in the morning and six in the evening, thus lessening the landlady's labour and affording her, if the truth be told, a profitable Box and Cox arrangement, whereby she could let the room in the daytime to a night watchman from the docks.

In this small house, the landlady, whose name was Haggitty, roomed seven people. She lingered at the door, her dirty hands folded over an apron even more grimy, to explain that she was very busy just now, her three "regulars" being in town.

"And I wouldn't offend the gentlemen for the world," she said. "They're away sometimes nine and ten months, and the money's paid as regular as clockwork...seafaring gentlemen – the captain of a ship, one is; the other two's his sons...as nice a man as ever drew the breath of life, when he's not in drink."

These privileged boarders had two rooms between them, the captain occupying the best (a poor best it was) at the front of the house.

"That's what I wanted to talk to you about, Mrs What's-your-name – "

"Brown," said Mrs Ollorby.

"I'm taking you in to oblige you," the woman went on, "but I don't want you to get in the way of the captain, because he's very short, and I wouldn't have him upset for a million pounds."

Apparently the captain's "shortness" was less of stature than temper. Sitting on her bed that night, reading a book by the light of a small electric lamp she had taken from her bag, Mrs Ollorby heard the uncertain steps of the captain on the stairs and the rumble of an unintelligible song. His ironshod feet clumped on the flimsy landing, and presently his door banged and the house shook with the shock of it.

Mrs Ollorby listened and waited for the arrival of the captain's family, but they did not come, and after a while she heard the lodger's door open and he came out. She waited till he had left the house, and then, putting down her book, she opened the door gently and listened. Silence reigned; there was no sound. The landlady had retired to a miserable truckle bed in the kitchen. Then a snore came up to her from the ground floor, where one of the lodgers slept...

Noiselessly, for she had changed her shoes for thick felt slippers, Mrs Ollorby crept across the landing, mounted the short flight of stairs that led to the upper landing, and tried the door of the privileged lodger. It was not locked. Pushing it open, she went into the room and turned on the light.

The room was a little better furnished than her own. There was a dressing-chest and a small table evidently used for writing, for a number of papers were scattered on its surface and there was a penny bottle of ink and a sheet of thin blotting paper. Rapidly she examined the documents, and found that they had to do with ships' stores, purchased a few days before. She inspected the bed, turned over the pillow, and discovered a flat worn note case, which contained, however, nothing more informative than a sheet of paper covered with figures. She had sufficient knowledge of the sea to realise that these represented a course that the captain had worked out. Against each position he had put a date, and she saw that the first of these was the 26th, and behind it was a query mark.

She replaced the paper and continued her search. As she did so she heard loud voices outside the window, and presently the grate of a key in the lock of the front door. Moving with surprising rapidity, she was out of the room in an instant, had closed the door and was behind her own before the first step sounded on the lower stair.

This time the captain was not alone; two men accompanied him. She heard them go into the captain's room and the door close quietly, and the sound of low voices speaking in an undertone. Softly she crept to the door, the crazy stairs creaking beneath her weight. Bending her head, she listened.

"...this man – what's his name? Waring something...the coon said...lay off Gravesend for the tide..."

Somebody moved across the floor. In a flash she was back in her room, her door ajar, listening. Eavesdropping was a dangerous business in this house, where every floorboard squeaked under her foot. After a quarter of an hour she heard two of the men come out and go into another room with a gruff "Goodnight, old man!" Closing her door softly, Mrs Ollorby lay down fully dressed on the bed, and in a few minutes was asleep.

It was the sound of the captain going downstairs that brought her wide awake. After a brief interval he was followed by his two sons. It was broad daylight now. Mrs Ollorby made a quick toilet, and in her turn descended to the street. She broke her fast at a coffee stall at the corner of Victoria Dock Road, and half an hour later was standing on a chill wharf, watching with interest a small, rusty steamer anchored in midstream. A waterside loafer slouched up to her, scenting a possible tip, which in the circumstances was more than justified, for he proved to be a mine of information.

"That little boat, missie? Want to get out to her? I can get you a boat in about five minutes."

"No," said Mrs Ollorby, "I don't want to get out to her."

"Got any relations on board?" asked the man, eager to serve. "Maybe you'd like to send a letter out to her?"

"What is she?" asked Mrs Ollorby.

"Her? She's the *Pretty Anne!*" He chuckled to himself. "That's a fancy name for a ship like that, ain't it? Yet I remember her when she was in the Cardiff trade and was as good a boat as ever came up Thames river. That's before she was wrecked down in Cornwall – went on the rocks – old Boss bought her for fifty pounds, they say, and him and his two sons floated her off – at least, she floated herself off at high tide."

That, then, was the history of the *Pretty Anne*. Wrecked, marked at Lloyd's as a total loss, and sold at junk price by auction to lucky Eli Boss. And a very lucky man was this Captain Eli Boss, for he had twice escaped penal servitude by the skin of his teeth, once for "wilfully casting away" and once for saccharine smuggling.

"Know him?" The loafer spat contemptuously in the water. "I should say I did! Who don't know Eli? He's a dog – he don't ship white men, just lascars and the riff-raff you can get at ten a penny. He's made money out of runnin' booze to America and money out of all sorts of dirty jobs. He never gets a decent cargo, because none of the underwriters will insure the ship."

"How does he make a living, then?" asked Mrs Ollorby.

The loafer spat again.

"He gets cargoes out of Bremen now and again," he explained. "Barrels of rum for the West Coast, or arms – he made a lot of money out of the Morocco war."

Mrs Ollorby looked at the ship with a new interest. An ungainly craft, with her discoloured hull, her high fo'c'sle deck and one stubby mast, she seemed out of proportion, a monstrosity of a ship, dingy, rusty, the paint on her funnel flaked away so that it seemed to be camouflage.

"The old man skippers her, one of the boys helps him, and the other's in charge of the engine-room. He's got a crew of six."

"What flag is he flying?" Mrs Ollorby had been interested by the small dirty square of bunting at the flagstaff.

"Portuguese. She wouldn't be allowed out of Thames river if she was registered in this country."

Apparently the *Pretty Anne* had her advantages, Mrs Ollorby learnt.

"She can do twelve knots, and I believe they can knock her up to fifteen, though I can't see old Eli spending the money for coal," said the informative lounger. "I never seen or heard she was ever in dock since the old man had her beached in Cornwall to put in new plates.

"She hasn't had any fires in her for a week," said the talkative longshoreman. "They say old Eli counts every bit of coal that goes into her furnace – that fellow is hot!"

Mrs Ollorby tipped him beyond his expectations, and, leaving the wharf, she found a telephone booth and was soon talking to her red-haired son.

"You come here straight away, Hector," she said. "Bring an overcoat, because the nights are chilly. I want you to do a bit of watching for me. And, Hector, listen: in my room, hanging up in the wardrobe, you'll find a pair of field-glasses; bring those with you."

She rang off and got another number, the Treasury number she had called from her house, and an interested police chief made copious notes at her dictation.

"Have you any idea what the game is?" he asked.

Mrs Ollorby hesitated.

"I'm full of ideas," she said cautiously.

"But facts are my weakness."

She waited for the greater part of an hour until her red-haired son came importantly to receive her instructions and money for sustenance. Fortunately, she was able to enlist the interest and assistance of the longshoreman, who, since he was in the habit of spending the year through with his hands in his pockets, looking at the river, from which occupation he apparently derived some sort of a living, was quite willing to take his turn with the boy.

"I don't suppose you'll see much, ma'am," he said. "The *Pretty Anne* won't be going down river for a week yet, from what one of the greasers told me; she hasn't got any cargo aboard, that I'll swear! Old Eli's bound to get a load of some sort before he fires up. I've never known the *Pretty Anne* to leave Thames river in ballast."

"A week or two means nothing to me," said Mrs Ollorby cheerfully, and she spoke the truth, for she was a woman of infinite patience.

8

A great regiment has great traditions, and one of the traditions of the Berwick Guards had to do with the eligibility of its officers' wives. No officer might marry an actress, however charming and popular, and remain on the Active List.

Bobbie Longfellow, who had been dining *en famille* with Colonel the Honourable John Ruislip and his wife, returned to his quarters in a somewhat chastened mood; for if the genial commander of the Berwick Guards took a somewhat lax view on the subject of eligibility, his austere wife (the third daughter of the Earl of Stanfield) supplied his deficiencies.

Bobbie, despite his youth, had a shrewd idea of worldly things, and because her ladyship had dropped a hint about the propriety of subalterns marrying out of their class, and particularly by reason of the fact that her comment had some special application, Mr Longfellow was just a little uneasy.

"The first essential to a successful marriage is Family," said her ladyship, fingering the big emerald ring that decorated her little finger. "If a gel hasn't Family, the marriage is a mistake."

A thin-lipped, spare and beautiful woman, she was never quite so definite as when she was twirling that big emerald about a finger just a little too small for it.

Bobbie was passing the door of Dick's quarters when he stopped, turned back and knocked at the door. Dick Hallowell's cheery voice bade him enter.

"Like Solomon in all his glory," murmured Dick, surveying with admiration the grand habit of his brother officer. "Been dining out, Bobbie?"

He himself had discarded his scarlet mess kit and, attired lightly in pyjamas and silken dressing gown, was poring over his company accounts. Bobbie selected a cigarette with infinite care before he answered.

"I've been grubbing with the old man," he said. "And the old woman," he added.

"Really, her ladyship is a terrifying person. She always gives me the impression that things have changed for the worse since she was a girl, and that I'm one of the things!"

Dick chuckled.

"Poor old Bobbie!" he said sympathetically. "I got over my official dinner more than a month ago."

"The Colonel isn't so bad," complained Bobbie, as he dropped into a deep-seated armchair and groped with his foot for another to rest his long legs. "And by the way, do you know that he's a friend of Diana's?"

Dick smiled.

"Diana has quite a number of friends – I seem to remember that they were acquainted in the old days. Did he boast of this?"

"He didn't tell me this before his missus," said Bobbie irrelevantly, "but he confided in me when we were alone over the logwood – "

"His port is the best in the regiment," protested Dick.

"Maybe it is," said Bobbie. "I was never a lover of ruby wine. It stodges my wonderful mind."

"Did the Colonel say anything about Diana?"

"He said she was a very charming girl," admitted Bobbie, "and it was such a pity her ladyship had cut her out of her visiting list. 'We all found her a very nice, charming soul' – you know the sort of stuff the old man would say in his fruity or expansive moments."

There was a long silence. Dick turned to his accounts and tried to fix his mind upon the long columns of figures. Presently Bobbie spoke again.

"She mentioned Miss Joyner," he said, and Dick swung round.

"Who – Lady Cynthia?"

Bobbie nodded.

"What had she to say about Miss Joyner?"

"Not much." The young man was obviously uncomfortable, but this discomfort was not communicated to Dick, who knew that Lady Cynthia Ruislip had precious little to say that was nice about any woman. "She was wondering who Miss Joyner was," said Bobbie, "and it didn't do much good when old John stepped gallantly into the breach and said she was one of the nicest girls he'd ever met, and even hinted that he knew her people."

Dick laughed softly.

"And what did the lady say?"

"You know what her attitude was likely to be. It's what she didn't say that made me grow hot under the collar. That trick of hers – raising her eyebrows and dropping the corners of her mouth – makes me want to scream. Of course she bowled out the old man in two twinks – found that he knew nothing whatever about Hope Joyner or her people, and really was very annoyed with him."

Dick went slowly back to his accounts, but though his pen was in his hand he did not write, as the other saw.

"I suppose – " began Bobbie, and stopped.

"You suppose what?" Dick did not turn his head.

"I suppose things are fixed up there all right?… I mean – "

"You mean between myself and Hope Joyner? There's nothing fixed, but I'm hoping desperately that she will think I am good enough for her. Why did you ask? A brain like yours should have discovered the fact ages ago."

Bobbie got up slowly and stretched his long limbs.

"I don't know," he said cautiously. "But I've an idea that old Cynthia has her knife into your young lady. Why, I haven't the slightest idea, except that she's got her knife into most people who can't trace their pedigrees back to the bloodthirsty old Plantagenets. By the way, the Colonel told me privately that he is dining with the rajah man."

"Kishlastan?" asked Dick, in surprise. "I didn't know they were friends."

"The Colonel met him in India apparently," explained Bobbie. "Anyway, he's dining tomorrow night, and he mentioned casually that Diana Martyn would be there – but he didn't say that before his wife."

"He's a rum devil – Kishlastan, I mean," frowned Dick Hallowell. "At the Foreign Office they say he's a little mad. The Under-Secretary was rather keen on my doing a little intelligence work for him."

Bobbie smiled. That anybody else should be asked to "do a little intelligence work" when he was available rather amused him.

Lieutenant Bobbie Longfellow, of the Berwick Guards, was, despite his somewhat vacuous appearance, a very shrewd young man; and if his shrewdness was tempered by illusion, that illusion was of a picturesque and romantic character.

It was Bobbie's ambition – fated one day to be realised – to enter the Military Intelligence Department of the War Office, and all his spare time was devoted to this fascinating study. He prided himself upon his detective qualities and, though he was not aware of the fact, had much in common with the red-haired son of Mrs Ollorby.

He went to his quarters after his interview with Dick, and sat for a long time turning over in his mind the unflattering estimate which Lady Cynthia had formed of the girl's eligibility for admission to the charmed society of the Berwick Guards. He knew enough of Hope Joyner to realise that she concealed nothing about herself, and that the mystery of her associations was as much a mystery to her as it was to the inquisitive outsiders. Here, then, was a most promising subject of investigation for a budding intelligence officer. Might he not, unaided, by sheer deduction and the maximum of luck, locate, in the forest of humanity, her particular family tree? For this is certain – that the meanest beggar that sweeps the streets has a pedigree of sorts leading back to Adam or to the lower animals which the evolutionists claim as their progenitors.

Unknown to his friend, he had already found a new interest in life; had made long and important excursions; interviewed all manner of genealogical experts – for he was a wealthy young man – and had bade them concentrate upon the 10th of June in an unknown year, for it was on the 10th of June that Hope Joyner received flowers from an unknown guardian.

9

The cottage at Cobham, as Graham Hallowell discovered when he went to take possession of his new hiring, justified the exorbitant rent (as he had considered it) demanded by the agent. As to this, since he had not to pay a cent, his indignation was a little unnecessary. It was a pretty little house in the Tudor style, standing in an acre or two of garden, and was isolated in the sense that there was no house within half a mile. The side road in which it stood was less than a quarter of a mile from the main Portsmouth Road, and it was more accessible from London than he had thought. It was the perfect summer cottage, with a glorious garden, blazing with colour, clumps of picturesque firs and a tiny bathing pool.

Diana did not accompany him to Cobham.

"If you dream that I am going to bury myself in the country, and moreover sprinkle ashes on my reputation, both you and Trayne are vastly mistaken," she said. "I will come down and lunch with you, and perhaps I'll stop to dinner, but beyond that – no!"

"I suppose you realise you're my wife?" said Graham sarcastically.

"I try not to, but in moments of depression I find it difficult to forget," said Diana steadily. "You also seem to forget that I have quite a number of duties in town."

Graham was more than a little in awe of this woman, with whom, by an act which both now regarded as of lunacy, he had joined himself. There was no love in this marriage, precious little respect. Folly and panic had driven them to the registrar's office one bitter December morning, and neither had ceased to regret their unnecessary precipitancy.

Graham went alone, wondering what arrangements had been made for his creature comfort. He found the house in charge of a gardener, a dour, uncommunicative man, who lived in a cottage on one corner of the small estate. The gardener's wife was cook and housemaid to the establishment, and she was assisted by her daughter, an unhappy-looking and, as Graham suspected, half-witted girl of sixteen.

The taciturn gardener showed him over the pretty little house, most of the rooms of which, Hallowell discovered, were locked up, leaving him a couple of bedrooms, the drawing and dining rooms and a small library so called, though it was innocent of books, for his own use. The sour gardener was respectful enough, though sparing of speech. His wife, though coarse and a little sinister of appearance, proved to be an excellent plain cook, and Graham settled himself down to a dull and comfortable time, though the rose garden promised a certain amount of interest to one who had a passion for flowers. The grounds were of greater extent than he had thought. They extended to a wilderness of pine and scrub, and behind the screen of the trees he came upon a curious structure.

It was a square stone tower, rising to the height of about thirty feet. There were no windows, and apparently the place was lit by electricity, for he saw a light cable fastened to the wall. A small door, so low that he would have been obliged to stoop had he entered, was let into one face.

A storehouse of some kind, he thought, and made the circuit of the building. There were no other doors to be seen, and he came back to the front of the building to find the gardener watching him interestedly.

"What place is that?" Graham asked.

The man surveyed the tower before he answered.

"An old granary," he said. "It isn't used nowadays."

"But you've had a power cable put in," suggested the visitor.

"Must have light," said the other indifferently. "It's cheaper than knocking windows through the walls."

There was nothing more said, and they went back to the house together. Graham dismissed the square stone building from his mind. Later he was to learn the important part it was to play in the great plan.

"Here is the key of the desk," said the gardener when they came to the study. "I'll get you a cup of tea."

He went out, closing the door behind him. Graham looked at the little key on the palm of his hand, and wondered why there had been this formal transfer, for it was the only key he had been given. And then a thought struck him, and he went to the little oaken desk, to find that every drawer was unlocked save one. He turned the key in this, pulled it open and saw that it contained a large square envelope, addressed to himself, a thick wad of stout large envelopes and three keys. The sealed envelope contained a smaller, which had in it twenty-five pound notes and a typewritten sheet of paper, bearing no signature and which began without preamble.

> The Crown Garage in the village will hire you a car. You may find this useful. Mawsey will garage it for you. Tomorrow night you had better go to the "Three Jolly Sailors" and get acquainted with Eli Boss, who will be expecting you. Go by car as far as Greenwich; leave the machine there and take a bus through the Blackwall Tunnel as far as Poplar. Make the rest of the journey on foot. Discuss nothing with Eli, your business being to establish touch with him. You are to accompany the fruit to India. He will ship you as a deck hand and will arrange for your kit. He has instructions to make you comfortable on board, so you had best tell him of your requirements. It is essential that you should have a cabin that can be locked inside and out. Get the best lock that money can buy and give it to him, but he is not to have the key. I have arranged for a small safe to be put in your cabin. E.B. thinks you are smuggling cocaine. He knows nothing about the fruit. After you have learnt details of the suggested operations, write out your own comments and leave

them in the desk where you found this letter, which must be burnt in the presence of Mawsey.

That was all, and when Mawsey (this seemed to be the gardener's name) brought in the cup of tea, Graham held the letter over the hearth, applied a match to a corner and watched it burn. No word was spoken. He realised that to attempt a conversation would be a profitless task, and when the man put his foot on the ashes and scattered them, he realised that the gardener knew as much about the contents of the letter as he did.

"Where is the 'Three Jolly Sailors'?" he asked.

Mawsey looked up from his task, brushed his foot carefully in the grate with a small hearth broom.

"I don't know any of the public houses around here," he said.

He had a reluctant way of talking, as though words were precious and he grudged their use.

"But when I was a boy I used to remember a house called the 'Three Jolly Sailors.' It was off Victoria Dock Road."

He went out of the room after this. Graham saw him pottering in the garden, and it seemed that whatever part Mr Mawsey was acting, he too had a genuine love of flowers. Indeed, when the new tenant of the cottage went out to join him he found the man almost human in his enthusiasm for a rare variety of aster he had succeeded in raising.

Mrs Mawsey served his dinner, and he was left alone until ten o'clock, when, with a preliminary knock, the gardener came into the room, shut the door behind him, and, diving into an inside pocket of his jacket, produced another sealed envelope. It was addressed "G. Hallowell," and when he had torn open the stout envelope he drew out the identical book he had seen in Tiger Trayne's hand.

Between the cover and the first page was a sheet of paper.

Before handing the book back to Mawsey it must be placed and sealed in one of the envelopes you will find in the third drawer of the writing bureau. This must be done every night. Burn these instructions.

Again Graham Hallowell carried out his orders under the watchful eye of the gardener.

"All right, Mawsey," he said, as he turned the leaves of the book. "I'll call you when I'm through."

The gardener shook his head.

"I'm very sorry, sir," he said harshly, "but I've got to be here all the time you're reading. He says you mustn't make notes or any copy."

"Who is 'he'?" asked Graham, curious to discover whether this servant would admit the identity of the Tiger.

"I don't know him by name," was the unpromising reply.

From ten until one o'clock Graham poured over the manuscript book. He read the book straight through at first, to get an idea of the general scheme. Not once but many times did he stop and gasp at the audacity of the plan. When he came to the end he turned back and read it slowly, page by page, memorising every particular. At one o'clock, when the typewritten characters were swimming under his eyes, he closed the book, searched for an envelope and sealed it up. Throughout those three hours Mawsey had sat stiffly, his hands on his knees, apparently untired by his ordeal. Once Graham had interrupted his reading to suggest that the man should smoke.

"I don't smoke and I don't drink," was the brief answer, and after that Hallowell went on, oblivious of the man's presence or the possibility of his discomfort.

The gardener took the sealed package, placed it carefully in his inside pocket, and, with a brief goodnight, turned to go.

"I shan't be here tomorrow night," said Graham.

"I know," was the man's answer.

Graham looked at him curiously.

"Our friend trusts you a lot," he said.

"He trusts you, sir; he has better reason to trust me," was the cryptic reply.

The next morning Hallowell went down to the village in search of books and newspapers, for time was already hanging heavily on his hands. He found the Crown Garage and hired a small coupé. That evening he drove leisurely to town, reached Greenwich soon after sunset, and made his way to the "Three Jolly Sailors."

There was little that was jovial in the appearance of the place. It was a dingy corner public-house, gas-lit and smelling; but it was a traditional meeting place for the rough men who sail the seas, and many a crew had been engaged on the sanded floor of the public bar, and, if the truth be told, many an unpleasant project had been rounded off in that section of the house which was magniloquently called the "saloon."

When Graham Hallowell pushed open the swing door and entered this latter sanctuary, he found that he was one of three occupants. A loafer sat in an old Windsor chair in one corner of the L-shaped bar, his hands clasped on his stomach, his hat pulled over his eyes, nodding and swaying in the first drowsiness of sleep. Against the zinc-covered counter stood a giant of a man, dressed in a rough pea-jacket over a blue jersey, a greasy peaked cap on the back of his grizzled head. A bristling grey moustache and a thick bush of iron-grey hair about throat and chin gave some regularity to a face that was otherwise without symmetry. Red, bloated, broken-nosed, the small eyes bloodshot, a most unprepossessing creature; Graham Hallowell, who had met with unbelievable ugliness of mind and body during his sojourn in Dartmoor, thought at any rate that he had never seen a human being so ill-favoured.

The big man favoured Graham with a quick glance as he came into the bar, but thereafter took no notice until: "Will you have a drink?" asked the newcomer.

The bloodshot eyes surveyed Graham for a second, and then: "Gin," he said briefly.

Captain Eli Boss was not a great conversationalist. Graham, at a loss as to how he would introduce himself, had to fall back upon the vagaries of the weather, a subject apparently in which the captain was not greatly interested. He drank down his gin and water, stretched himself...

"I'll be going home," he said. "Maybe you'd like to walk my way, sir?"

He had a deep, hoarse voice that seemed to come from some subterranean cavern of speech, and he scarcely glanced at the other when he issued this invitation. Graham nodded and followed the man outside. They walked for a long way in silence, moving in the direction of Silvertown, and it was not until they had reached a lifeless slum street that the big man spoke.

"The governor says you'll want a lock on your cabin door – it's a waste of money, but you can have it, and a safe. Send 'em both to Tigley's in Little Perch Street; he does my stores. I'll make you as comfortable as I can, but the *Pretty Anne* ain't no *Mauretania*, and don't you forget it – plain food and plenty of it, that's my motto. Do you play euchre?"

Graham did not play euchre, and the captain grunted his disapproval at this neglect of his education.

"You'd better bring some books," he said. "Me and my boys don't read much."

"When do you expect to sail?" asked Graham.

Eli Boss shot a sideways glance at him.

"When do *you*? That's the question," he growled. "Round about the twenty-sixth?"

Hallowell, who had no idea of the date, realised with a pang of dismay that the twenty-sixth was close at hand.

"I suppose so," he said.

"She jumps about a bit in the sea" – the captain was evidently reverting to the *Pretty Anne* – "but I'd class her A1 in any kind of weather. Give me a ship that moves – these stiff packets get all buckled up in a cross sea...plenty of food; but plain. There's nothing fancy about the *Pretty Anne*. And listen – you'd better bring your own liquor aboard. Gin's all I want, and a glass of rum for a cold watch. I've cleared out Joe's cabin – he's my engineer – amidships, abaft the bridge. It's the best pitch in the ship, but hot as hell in the tropics."

"I could get an electric fan," suggested Hallowell, and the man guffawed deeply.

"Electric nothing!" he snapped. "Because why? There ain't no electric on the boat – nothing fancy. Oil's good enough for me. I got a dynamo, but she won't work – dynamos means steam, and steam means coal, and coal's money."

He had a trick of going off at a tangent and of returning without warning to something he had said before.

"Joe can bunk with me, and Fred can get a shakedown in the chart house," he said. "They like their own cabins, but you can't always get what you want."

"Am I turning both out?"

"You're turning out Joe," said Captain Boss. "I want Fred's cabin for – "

Graham heard the click of his jaws as they snapped together, as though, conscious of an indiscretion, he was physically inhibiting the statement he had begun.

"What are you running 'coke' to India for?" demanded Eli. "Bremen's the place for 'coke' – you can get it by the ton. I took a million dollars' worth out to Buenos Aires and it was easy."

He stopped at the end of the street, thrust his hands deep into his pockets and looked down at his companion.

"I'll be going now," he said. "Don't forget Tigley's in Little Perch Street. Fred'll fix the lock for you." He paused, as though he were trying to remember something he had to say, and then, with a brief "So long!" he crossed the road.

Graham was not well acquainted with Canning Town, and to be on the safe side he walked back the way he had come.

At the end of the long and dreary street he branched off towards Victoria Dock Road, and came to this comparatively busy thoroughfare as the local picture palace was disgorging its patrons. He made his way with some difficulty through the throng, crossed the railway bridge, and waited on the sidewalk for the bus that would carry him through the Blackwall Tunnel.

There was a stopping-place here, where buses pull up to collect their passengers, and he found that he had overshot the mark and, turning, walked leisurely back. He had nearly reached the little knot of people who were waiting for a similar reason, when he came almost face to face with a stout woman. She turned quickly, but not quickly enough. In the light of a street lamp he saw the large, powerful nose and the unmistakable chin of one whom he recognised immediately. And, recognising her, his pulse beat a little faster. It was Mrs Ollorby!

10

He went back to Greenwich, collected his car, and, instead of driving back to Cobham, he found a telephone booth that was accessible at that hour of the night, and called the Mousetrap number. Mr Trayne was on the premises, it seemed, and in a remarkably short time was speaking to him.

"I've seen a friend of ours," said Graham cautiously. "Do you remember the woman we saw when we looked out of the window?"

"Mrs O?" was the quick reply, and when Graham had affirmed this: "Where was she?"

"In Canning Town. I've an idea she was trailing me."

It was a long time before Trayne spoke.

"Come west; pick me up along Wardour Street. Your car's a closed one, isn't it? Good! I'll be waiting for you in twenty minutes."

Graham continued his journey, and in a deserted stretch of Wardour Street overtook his employer and slowed his car long enough for the man to jump in.

"Regent's Park – the Outer Circle," ordered Trayne, and did not speak until they were slowly circling that desolation.

"Now tell me about this woman."

"There's little to tell," said Graham with a rueful laugh. "I didn't see her until I was waiting for the bus, but I'm pretty certain she was watching me all the evening."

Another long and thoughtful silence.

"I wonder what she knows?" mused Trayne. "She was not in the 'Jolly Sailors' when you were there?"

Graham shook his head.

"I should have recognised her at once," he said. "No, I think she must have picked me up after I left the captain – I'll swear there was nobody in the street where I was talking with him."

"Humph!" Trayne was not convinced. "The fat woman, she's wonderful," he said with reluctant admiration. "I wouldn't like to swear that she hasn't had you under observation from the moment you left Cobham. What do you think of Eli?" he asked abruptly.

"The captain? He's not a very beautiful specimen."

"There's nothing in him except his usefulness," said Trayne. "He's the type who would double-cross his only son. He has done work for me before, but nothing like this. There's one point I must warn you against: he must not know what you're carrying to India, or the stuff will never get there. So long as he thinks it is cocaine, there is no danger."

"Is he likely to know?"

Trayne shook his head.

"Not unless the ship is stopped in the Channel. He makes a show of carrying wireless, but I happen to know that it's a dummy set, put up to satisfy the requirements of our Board of Trade – he has been chartered before now by an English firm. When you send your trunks aboard, you'd better pack a couple of guns and a hundred rounds or so – you may want them."

"Does he know you're in this?" asked Graham curiously, and to his surprise the older man returned a decisive "No."

"He thinks he's 'obliging' a friend of mine. Eli does everything to oblige. That is his complex – that he is doing people a favour. He's a brute, but his form of brutality won't worry you very much."

"What is the form?" asked Graham.

"Women," was the laconic reply. "He's been before the magistrates three times, and he had a narrow squeak of going down for a long term as a result of an affair he had with a girl in Truro. You wouldn't think it possible, but Eli is under the impression that he's a fine figure of a man, rather beautiful to look upon! That's the form his insanity takes, and his sons are as bad – worse, because they encourage the old devil in his vanity. In that respect he is about as wholesome as fungus. Money is his god, but the only thing that will ever trip him up in his worship is something feminine. Happily, you won't have that complication, for it is part of his contract with me, or rather with my mythical friend, that a woman is not to cross the gangway, and the price he is being paid is big enough to make him keep to his agreement."

He did not speak again of Mrs Ollorby, and soon after Graham set him down in Gower Street and made the best of his way home. It was very late when he arrived, but the gardener was waiting up for him, and greeted him on the doorstep with a question.

"Did you expect a phone call round about eleven o'clock?"

"I?" said Hallowell, in surprise. "No – why?"

"Were you expecting a message from your wife?"

"No, it is very unlikely she would call me up. I don't think she knows the number."

"Somebody knows it all right," said the gardener. "You were called up at eleven o'clock – by a woman. She gave your own name and asked when you were expected back."

"What did you say?"

"I told her I didn't know who she was talking about. She wouldn't tell me who she was, but she left a message. I've written it down."

Graham followed him into the study, and on the blotting pad was a sheet of paper on which, written in an irregular boyish hand, was the message

There is no safe as secure as Room 79, B Ward.

Graham Hallowell went white to the lips. For 79 was the number of the cell he had occupied, and B Ward was one of the radiating blocks in that little hell which is called Dartmoor Convict Establishment.

11

The Prince of Kishlastan could give parties which were vulgar in their ostentation and splendour, but he could also arrange dinners which were exquisite in their taste. His Excellency, in immaculate evening dress and undistinguishable from any other gentleman save for the copper skin and the white turban about his head, walked into the panelled dining room of his private suite and inspected the table.

Mr Colley Warrington, who had arrived half an hour before the first of the guests was due, nodded his expert approval as he examined one of the menu cards.

"That will tickle the Colonel," he said, his thumbnail against an item in the short but perfect wine list.

The Prince pursed his thin lips.

"So far as I am concerned, the dinner will be a bore. I am quite sure that Miss Joyner could have been induced to come if sufficient trouble had been taken," he said pettishly.

"You're wrong, Excellency," said Colley, with a quiet smile. "It would have been the worst of tactics to have invited her. She would have refused, of course, but the invitation would have made it impossible for me to have got any farther in her – er – little matter."

"You didn't even write to her!" said Rikisivi ill-temperedly. "You have left her with the impression that we have – what shall I say? – given her up as a bad job – that we are so ashamed because of the pearls, that we dare not meet her again. And I want her here – I want her here! She is necessary for me. When I do not see her, I am unhappy. If you had written – "

"I did write," said Colley, his attention apparently occupied with the setting of the table, for he did not look at His Excellency as he spoke. "I told her you were giving a little dinner party, and that Hallowell's Colonel would be amongst the guests, but that I didn't think she would care to come."

"Ten thousand devils!" snarled the Prince. "Why did you tell her that, you fool?"

"Because," said Colley calmly, "it was necessary to give her the impression that you have a delicate care for her reputation. For I added that Diana would be here, and that I didn't think she would like to meet her."

"But Diana need not have come!" exploded Riki.

"Of course she need not," said the other coolly. "But by so writing I have placed little Joyner under an obligation. She must either write and say that in no circumstances, whether Diana was here or not, would she accept your invitation, or else, when I invite her again, she must accept."

"And when do you intend inviting her again?" Kishlastan was more than a little irritated.

"After you have left for the East, Excellency," said Colley slowly. "And you will leave for the East a few days before I dine with Hope Joyner. It is vitally necessary," he went on, "that you should not be in town when – things happen. You must be on the seas, with a whole ship's company of the P & O Line to testify to your innocence."

The Prince considered this.

"Do you think you will succeed?"

"I am certain to succeed," said Colley. "And may I suggest to your Excellency that there is another reason why you should leave? I do not wish to pry into your affairs, nor do I seek further information than that which you have been graciously pleased to give me concerning a certain enterprise which is in the hands of a friend. But I do say this: that it would be advisable if you left before the fulfilment of that little plan."

"I am leaving a week after," said the other impatiently. "I cannot leave at a moment's notice; I require very large accommodation for my suite."

"Which I," said Colley carefully, "have reserved on the *Poltan*, which leaves on Saturday."

The Prince stared at him, half angry, half amazed.

"You may regard that as an impertinence on my part, but I have your interests to serve, and I took the trouble this afternoon to discover where accommodation was available. Fortunately, a big reservation on the *Poltan* had fallen through, and very promptly I made a provisional booking for your Excellency."

The Prince bit his lip thoughtfully.

"Perhaps you are right," he said. "You are a very far-seeing and cunning man. I will discuss this matter with you after these people have gone."

They had not been back in the saloon ten minutes when the first of "these people" arrived – Diana, radiantly beautiful, the infatuated Colley thought, in a grey silvery gown which somehow toned her mature beauty to a youthfulness that even the Prince could admire. She went into the dining room to take a quick look at the table, changed two of the cards and came back to tell them what she had done.

"I want to sit next to the Colonel," she said. "If you put Jane Lyson there she will bore him to tears. What's more, she hates his wife, and she couldn't resist the temptation of telling him so."

"Should I have invited Lady Cynthia?" asked His Excellency dubiously.

"She wouldn't have come," said the practical Diana, "not if she knew I was here. And I particularly wish to see the Colonel."

The conversation was interrupted by the arrival of an Indian official and his young and bejewelled wife, and soon after came Colonel Ruislip, who, when not attended by her ladyship, was a very jovial, not to say boisterous, quantity.

"Bless my life, Diana!" he said, holding her at arm's length and gazing admiringly into her smiling eyes. "You're younger than ever! What a fool Dick Hallowell was, to be sure!"

Nobody knew better than the Colonel that Dick Hallowell's folly was well occasioned, and his protest was but one of those pieces of polite and wilful blindness to facts which go to garnish the amenities of society.

"Hullo, Colley! Haven't seen you for years." He offered a limp and half-hearted hand to the spruce worldling. For, whatever Colonel Ruislip might be, he was no fool. Colley Warrington was one of those men whom one meets but never seeks. "I must have a chat with you, Colley…haven't heard real scandal for years."

Had the success of the dinner depended upon the cheerfulness and bonhomie of their host it would have been a sad affair, for His Excellency sulked without disguise, and scarcely spoke to the important lady on his right throughout the meal.

"Dick? Why, yes, I see a lot of Dick, of course."

"A very good officer," said the Colonel, sipping his wine with the grimaces peculiar to a connoisseur. "Thank God we rescued him from those flying people! I suppose you know he wanted to transfer into the Flying Corps after – hum – your little trouble? And a jolly good flier he is, too, by all accounts. He took me up at Aldershot and scared the life out of me. Give me solid ground beneath my feet – preferably my horse's hoofs…"

"He is engaged again, isn't he?"

The Colonel was a little uneasy.

"I couldn't tell you, my dear. I never bother about subalterns' engagements until they come to a head, so to speak. Standing *in loco parentis* to the battalion, they have to toddle along and tell me sooner or later – I've had no official intimation."

"You will have," said Diana sweetly. "Miss Hope Joyner – do you know her?"

"Met her – yes, I've met her," said the Colonel airily, and tried to change the subject. "Deuced pretty girl. Her ladyship was only saying the other day…"

But Diana redirected him from the realm of fiction to which he was heading.

"I hope Dick will be very happy," she said, in that tone of sweet resignation which the subject demanded.

"I'm sure," murmured the Colonel.

He added something about Hope being an acquisition to the regiment.

"Will she be?" asked Diana innocently, and the Colonel moved uncomfortably on his chair.

"Why, yes, I think so," he said hastily. "Very pretty…charming gel…"

And then, in his anxiety to make the conversation less personal, he fell into the trap that Diana had laid.

"Who are her people, by the way?"

Diana Martyn could now afford to concentrate her attention upon her plate.

"Has she any?" she asked.

"Dead?" asked the Colonel. "Tut tut! What a pity!"

"One doesn't even know they're dead," said Diana, and, fearful that his interest should flag : "And nobody knows less than Hope."

The old man frowned.

"That is rather a serious thing to say," he said quietly.

Diana shrugged her shapely white shoulders.

"It is the truth," she said. "There is nothing more serious than that."

Very briefly she sketched the history of Hope Joyner, and although she presented a faithful story, the sinister possibilities of Hope's beginnings lost nothing for want of emphasis.

"Of course, Dick could not possibly remain in the regiment after he married her," Diana prattled on. "I don't suppose he'd want to, anyway – "

"On the contrary, he intends to remain in the regiment," said the Colonel gruffly. "His captaincy is due next month, and I know it is his wish to command the battalion, as his father did before him. There has been a Hallowell in the Berwick Guards ever since it was formed."

"Then you'll have to be without a Hallowell for a while," she said gaily. "It really is impossible, don't you think, Colonel?"

He did not answer. For one member of the party at least, the evening was spoilt.

When he picked up the conversation again, it was to refer to a subject that Diana would gladly have avoided.

"Dick has had quite enough trouble with his blackguard of a half-brother," he said, "without having this dumped upon him. The girl is very charming, a lady, and I should be perfectly satisfied with Dick's assurance – "

She glanced at him shyly.

"Of course you would," she cooed. "And Lady Cynthia – ?"

She saw him wince, and knew that her point had reached home.

When all the guests save she and Colley had gone that night, the rajah, who had grown a little more cheerful as the evening progressed, asked: "You were talking about Hope Joyner to the Colonel: what did you say about her?"

Diana smiled.

"What could I say except that she is very charming and very sweet?" she asked innocently. "Really, I wasn't talking so much about her as of Dick Hallowell. Richard is thinking of marrying her."

She saw his face change.

"Marrying?" He turned to Colley. "I didn't know."

"There is some sort of attachment," said Colley. "I don't think they are engaged."

"He is in love with her," said Diana lightly, "and that is almost tantamount to an engagement. They're both well off and both otherwise heart free. Why shouldn't they be engaged? Dick Hallowell will have to leave his regiment, of course. The Berwick ladies will never allow a nobody to come amongst them."

"What do you mean by 'a nobody'?" demanded Riki, looking at her from under his lowered brows. "Nobody? Is Miss Joyner a nobody?"

"Oh la la!" Diana simulated an amusement she did not feel. "How very annoyed you sound, Excellency! And yet you should be the first to realise how very important birth can be – you who come down without a break in your ancestry for a thousand years."

He was mollified with this, being insanely proud of his lineage.

"It is to me," he said, "not wise to speak unkindly of Miss Joyner. There are many reasons why it should not be done. You agree?"

Colley nodded.

"There must be no suggestion that anybody who is remotely associated with Kishlastan is in the slightest degree antagonistic."

"Absolutely," said Colley, and the girl looked at him in astonishment.

"Is there any very special scheme connected with Hope Joyner?" she began.

"None whatever," said Colley promptly, "but I quite agree with His Excellency: we do not wish to make enemies. Your whole *raison d'être* is to enlarge his circle of friends. You must be charitable even to your rivals."

If he hoped to irritate her, he was to be disappointed. She was too absorbed in the new problem. There was a scheme on foot that concerned Hope Joyner, and she was not in it. To ask Colley for further information would be useless, as she knew. Perhaps Graham was in the plot.

Early the next morning, when the milkmen were still clattering their bottles in the street, she telephoned for her little car and drove to Cobham, and arrived to find Graham sitting before a cold and untasted breakfast. He looked up with a start as she came in.

"Oh, it's you, is it?" he said. "We're honoured."

A glance at his face set her wondering. His skin had that greenish tint which she had seen once before – the morning of his arrest.

"What is troubling you?" she asked.

"Nothing." He leaned over and pulled out a chair for her. "Pour out some coffee, will you? I haven't the energy."

She sat down without a word, filled and passed a cup to him, her eyes never leaving his face.

"What is the matter?" she asked again.

"Nothing very much." He glanced round at the door that she had left ajar, rose and closed it before he came back and told her in a low tone of his experience on the previous night.

When he had finished she shook her head.

"No, I sent you no telephone message. It was that wretched woman."

"But she knew I was in London," he insisted.

Diana smiled.

"Of course she knew you were in London, and equally of course she knew that the message she sent to you would be written down and handed to you on your return. It is awfully hard to believe that she's a detective, but I suppose she is no more commonplace than the male of the species."

She knit her brows in thought. Diana was a clever woman, infinitely quicker, more resourceful and possessing a greater courage than the man with whom fate had linked her.

"Where were you when he told you about the safe?"

"It was Trayne who told me. This sea captain certainly referred to the safe, but we were standing where it was impossible that anybody could have overheard us."

She nodded slowly.

"Nobody could have read the letter except the gardener."

Then suddenly she smiled.

"She got it from Trayne. She knows that he's bought a safe and that he has ordered it to be delivered to Captain Boss. That's the explanation."

"But how did she know it had to do with me?"

"It's simple," said Diana calmly. "Mrs Ollorby saw you with Boss; she knows the safe has been ordered for delivery to the – what is the name of the ship? – the *Pretty Anne*. It was merely a matter of putting two and two together. Probably she sent this message to make sure. When you had it, did you call up Trayne?"

He nodded.

"Of course you did! And she had somebody listening in. Was Trayne there?"

"He was out," said Graham.

"And a lucky thing for you he was!" she warned him. "I'm not worried about Mrs Ollorby: she's a guesser. She may guess right, but she isn't quite sure she is right. I've got one piece of advice to give you – keep away from the telephone; don't get rattled – "

There was a tap at the door, and before Graham could bid the man enter, the gardener slipped into the room and closed the door behind him.

"Do you know a Mrs Ollorby?" he asked in a low voice.

Too astonished for words, Graham Hallowell nodded.

"Do you want to see her?"

"See her?" Diana asked in amazement. "Why?"

"She's outside."

They looked at one another, Graham and his wife.

"Do you want to see her?" asked the gardener again.

Diana was the first to recover from the paralysis with which this astounding news had struck them.

"Where? In here?"

"Here," she said, and when Graham opened his mouth to protest, she silenced him with a gesture.

A second passed, the door opened quickly and Mrs Ollorby, all beaming smiles and radiating cheerfulness, exploded into the apartment.

"Good morning, people!" Her tone was offensively cheerful; she displayed none of that servility which had distinguished her first encounter with Diana. Rather she spoke as equal to equals. "What a blessed thing is the sunlight and the little flowers! Lord, the trees and the leaves rustling – it makes me feel a girl again! Some people like the sea," she rattled on, "but give me the countryside, the lawns and the 'erbaceous borders!" (Only occasionally was her English at fault.) "And the twisty chimneys! Ships have got chimneys, too – nasty black things with the paint peeling off them – but they haven't got pine trees and rock gardens, have they, Miss Martyn?"

Diana did not answer.

"The best thing about a ship," Mrs Ollorby continued without encouragement, "is its name – which means nothing. Now take the *Pretty Anne* for instance: is there anything pretty about her? Not even her skipper! I'd sooner be living in this cottage with a cash box than roving the Atlantic Ocean with a safe. Especially if I were a gentleman who'd had a little bit of trouble. Don't you agree, Miss Martyn?"

The gardener was still standing by the door, as petrified as any by this unexpected apparition. But now Diana found her voice, and with a laugh she began: "I'm at a loss – "

But the woman interrupted.

"You're at a loss to understand what I mean by barging into your pretty little house?" said Mrs Ollorby, smiling broadly. "Do you know, Miss Martyn, I was just wondering how you'd start – whether it would be 'I am at a loss' or whether it would be 'Will you kindly explain,' or just 'How dare you?' When you come to think of it, there's very little original you can say when you're annoyed, because, if you've got intelligence enough to think out something new, you've got intelligence enough to keep your temper."

She looked round the dining room with its panelled walls, its blue china against the rough-cast of frieze, the polished table with its bowl of roses, the dimity curtains gently swaying at the casement windows in the light morning breezes.

"It's a nice little house," she said, nodding her head emphatically. "I've seen it before, of course. Tiger Trayne let it to Johnny Delbourne – you know Tiger's the owner, of course? – before Johnny did that bank robbery. You must have met him in Dartmoor, Mr Hallowell. He got twenty years. I often wonder Tiger doesn't give up the Mousetrap Club and end his declining days here. Probably there are no mice worth catching."

She turned her head, met the gardener's glazed eyes and nodded familiarly.

"Mr Mawsey, isn't it? It used to be Colter, and then it used to be Wilson – I've almost lost track of your names, but I remember your convictions. How is that good lady, your wife?" She looked at his green apron and nodded. "Gardening – an old profession; or maybe farming. More profitable for Mrs Mawsey, or Wilson, or whatever your name was, than baby-farming."

She turned her merry eyes upon the pallid Diana, and, with a sinking at heart, the girl saw Mawsey slip through the door and disappear. Mrs Ollorby waited as though for some further remark from her unwilling hostess, but Diana was too wise to speak.

"It's a wonderful place, this," said Mrs Ollorby, shaking her head in an ecstasy of admiration. "But if I had all that ground, I think I'd keep chickens. There's nothing like a hobby – keeping something. I've kept scrapbooks ever since I was a young girl. It used to give my mother the horrors to see me cutting out crimes from the Sunday papers and sticking 'em into exercise books. I've got piles of 'em, so high" – she indicated the height of her shoulder. "I always thought I should marry a policeman, though I never dreamt I should work for Scotland Yard. Hector – that's my boy, and as good a boy as ever lived, though a little short-sighted – often says: 'Ma, what do you keep the scrapbooks for, when you carry them all in your mind?' And I do, that's a fact. It only seems yesterday that I stood in the Old Bailey and saw – what does he call himself? Mawsey? – go down for five. Mawsey's a good safe-breaker, one of the best. They say he's got a process for cutting through steel which got all the American gangs guessing. It makes you proud of your country, doesn't it, Miss Martyn?"

"Why are we honoured by your presence this morning?" asked Diana, mistress of herself at last.

"I wanted fresh air – badly," said Mrs Ollorby. "The truth is, I've been living in a slum for two days, in a dingy little back street. Not even the company of Captain Eli Boss was compensation – I'm full of long words this morning – for being stifled. So I said to Hector: 'I'll run along to Cobham and see Miss Martyn, or Mrs Halowell, as the case may be, and perhaps I'll kill two birds with one stone and save her an awful lot of trouble. And Mr Hallowell, too.' "

She smiled quizzically at the white-faced Graham.

"What is rattling you people" – she shook her head sadly – "is it that you don't know quite how much I know! I know nothing more rattling. You can't be sure how much I'm guessing and how much I'm reading out of a book, so to speak."

"We've heard of you, Mrs Ollorby." It was Graham who spoke.

"I'm getting famous." Mrs Ollorby almost smirked. "And that's curious, because I very seldom go into the witness box, and I don't suppose you'd have known me at all, only Tiger-tiger introduced me. I saw you all at the window and guessed – I'm a good guesser, as I say."

"You're not exactly, modest." Graham Hallowell was getting back to normal. "And you're certainly not amusing. Anyway, you're not amusing me. If you've any business you had better tell us what it is. If you haven't any business we'll excuse you."

"Always polite," murmured Mrs Ollorby. "You might almost be the Prince of Kishlastan, who never kills a Nautch girl but he takes off his hat first. Are you thinking of taking a long voyage, Mr Hallowell?"

Graham got up from the table, opened the door and pointed towards the garden path.

"You want me to go? I'm afraid I'm boring you, yet I'm usually considered rather entertaining. Hector says he could listen to me for hours; but then, of course, he's my own son. Good morning, Mrs Hallowell."

Diana did not reply to the little curtsy.

"Good morning, Mr Graham Hallowell."

He closed the door in her face, and Mrs Ollorby went striding down the crazy path, humming a little tune, a broad smile on her face. A stranger would have been excused had he imagined that she was taking leave of somebody who had amused her intensely.

They watched her through the leaded windows till her nodding bonnet vanished beyond the hedge, and then they looked at each other again in silence.

"What does she know?" asked Diana quietly.

"I can't guess. Not a lot, or she'd have been more explicit," he said thoughtfully. "Her job is not to arrest but to warn."

Diana nodded.

"She has got hold of two or three loose threads, and she is trying to make us connect them up," she said. "Captain Boss – that's the man who owns the ship, isn't it? Then you did see this woman in the East End last night, and of course it was she who telephoned. But she doesn't know, Graham: she's guessing, but she doesn't know. Didn't you see how all the time she was waiting for you or for me to blurt something which would connect up the loose ends?"

There was a soft tap on the door and the gardener came in, his lean face twitching.

"Is she gone?" he asked huskily.

"Do you know her?" demanded Diana.

"I know of her." Mawsey was not inclined to commit himself. "I knew her husband better: he was a detective sergeant at Scotland Yard. He – " The man hesitated – "He nearly got my wife into very serious trouble, and she was as innocent as a babe unborn."

"She seems to have got you into trouble once or twice."

"Not she, her husband," corrected Mawsey.

"I suppose it is all true?"

He met Diana's questioning glance with a nod.

"Oh, yes, I've been in quod," he said without embarrassment. "I wonder what she knows – guessing's her long suit: I suppose you've heard of that? But she's guessed a good many men into jail because they've been fools enough to give themselves away the first time they were tackled by her. You didn't say anything, did you?" he asked quickly, and, when they shook their heads together: "I didn't think you would. That old woman is poison, and don't forget it. She can do things that a he-policeman wouldn't dare do, and get away with it. Now what did she say? I want to tell the governor; he'll be calling up in a few minutes."

As faithfully as possible, Diana related the gist of the conversation.

"She's got a few things right," agreed Mawsey, "but she hasn't an inkling of the big scheme. She's just seen you fooling around with Eli Boss, she knows you've called on the governor, and she's guessed all her connections."

Without so much as "by your leave" he walked to the window and looked out.

"She's not gone," he said in a low voice. Wonder what she's waiting for?"

Mrs Ollorby had crossed the road and was standing under a large overhanging tree, looking back towards the house. In her hand was a white piece of paper, and alternately she looked and read. Suddenly Diana saw the gardener stiffen.

"She's going across Rectory Field," he said, and, looking round, saw that the stout woman had vanished. "I'll give that old cat the scare of her life."

He was out of the room in a flash, and a few seconds later Graham saw him running across the road with a gun under his arm; and as he ran he rammed home two shells in the breech.

The path across Rectory Field is a short cut to the main Esher Road, but it is one of those circuitous short cuts which have dubious advantages as time-savers. The track, a little better, that Mawsey followed skirted a plantation of firs, and he slackened his pace as he came to the corner of the copse, moving more cautiously. Presently he saw her; she was striding along the yellow path, not more than twenty yards away from him. With a grin he lifted his gun to his shoulder and the two barrels exploded. The shots went high, for he intended no more than a scare; and when the bonnet ducked, he could have rolled with laughter. But only for a second. The big reticule that she carried under her arm dropped; something appeared in her hand.

Pang!

He stood, frozen to inactivity, as he saw the red flame leap from her hand. The bullet smacked against the smooth bole of a young tree and went humming past his ear. He leapt out into the open, waving his hands wildly.

"Hi! What are you doing?" he yelled.

Mrs Ollorby came towards him, Browning in hand, a genial smile stretching her broad face.

"Don't tell me you thought I was a bird," she said, raising her hand in expostulation. "I am a bird in the vulgar sense – an old bird – but one of the birds that shoot back."

"What in hell are you doing?" gasped the man, who was as pale as death. "Just having a joke with you...thought I'd scare you, that's all..."

"Am I laughing?" demanded Mrs Ollorby, her big hand on her hips, the barrel of the automatic sticking out sideways, absurdly, like a foreshortened tail.

She was a ludicrous, almost an offensive, sight. Her bonnet had slipped rakishly over one eye; her red face was redder and moist. She was a woman of many chins, and now he had the illusion that, like the pouter pigeon, indignation had produced a collar of angry flesh. But she was laughing, and she was anything but scared, as she reminded him.

"If I thought it was wilful murder you were after, I'd be showing you the way to Kingston police station now, my man. But I see that it was just natural funniness."

She pushed her bonnet straight; fingered back a wisp of hair that had strayed down over her broad forehead, and examined her powder-blackened hand.

"Be good," she said abruptly, and, turning, walked back to where she had dropped her big bag.

He stood, rooted to the spot, until she had disappeared behind the thick plantation of Sutton Holme. Then he went back to find a worried Graham standing in the road.

"What did you do?" demanded Graham roughly.

"Just went to scare her," growled the man.

"Scare her! I heard three shots – ?"

"She had a gun," said the man sulkily. "And listen, Hallowell, you needn't tell the governor anything about this."

Graham made no such promise, but rejoined Diana in the morning room and explained the extent of the gardener's jest. Diana nodded slowly.

"This is where I go home, quick," she said. "The old theory that all criminals are fools seems to hold good. Shall I tell Tiger, or will you?"

"You had better," said Graham. "If this is the kind of assistance he's depending on, he can't know too soon."

Diana left soon after, and reached her flat, to find the very man she most desired to see. She was a little surprised, however, that Tiger should commit the indiscretion of calling on her in broad daylight. It was the first visit he had made to her flat, and she was a little worried. He must have read her concern in her face as she came into the drawing room to find him sitting on a couch, reading an illustrated paper.

"I've also got a flat in this block," he said surprisingly. "I've had it for two years. The police know, though apparently you don't. What's this trouble with Mawsey?"

"How did you know?" she asked in amazement.

"Your husband called me up – I wish he was not quite as handy with that phone of his. I'm moving Mawsey: he's a good workman but a bad thinker. I don't suppose any harm has come from the fool trick he played on Ollorby, but he'll be useful on the twenty-sixth, and it's best to get him away where he can't be picked up."

"Mr Trayne, why do you employ a man like that?"

He smiled good-humouredly, and Tiger Trayne had rather a beautiful smile.

"He is a good workman, as I said before, and I'm under some obligation to his wife – a slight one, it is true, and she isn't aware of the fact. Loyalty is my weakness."

She was nibbling at her nails, deep in thought.

"You said the twenty-sixth?"

He nodded.

"That's awfully soon."

"I didn't know until this morning that that was the day on which Richard Hallowell commands the guard."

Her mouth opened wide in surprise. "Richard Hallowell? What has that to do with it?"

"Everything," he replied. "You haven't read the book?"

She shook her head.

"And I suppose friend Graham had no time to explain things to you. The twenty-sixth suits for many reasons. There is the right kind of tide and the right kind of moon – which means there will be no moon at all – and, moreover, it's a few days before the State opening of Parliament, when the regalia will be required. I don't know what the weather will be like; I can only hope that it rains."

"You're taking the gardener away, then?"

He nodded.

"I should have taken him away, anyhow," he said. "I want a different kind of man there from now on – somebody who is a good tailor."

In spite of her anxiety she was surprised into a laugh.

"Why a good tailor? And, Mr Trayne," she said as she remembered, "you promised me a very substantial sum. What have I to do for it?"

He looked at her quizzically.

"Your task is a very simple one. I want you to dine with Lady Cynthia Ruislip."

Diana stared at him.

"Dine – I?" She laughed scornfully. "Do you realise what Lady Cynthia Ruislip would say to me? What sort of message the servant would bring? That idea is absurd; I can do nothing there."

He got up from the sofa, folded the paper carefully and replaced it on the table where he had found it.

"On the contrary, you can do a great deal. You were engaged to Graham Hallowell's brother, weren't you?"

She nodded.

"A good fellow?" he asked. "I don't know anything about him, except that he's one of the leisured and honest classes."

"He is – " she began, but he stopped her with a wave of his hand.

"I want to know nothing about him except how he looks in uniform, and I know that. I have twenty snapshots of him taken at various times without his knowing very much about it. But in your capacity as his fiancée you met Lady Cynthia?"

"Yes," said Diana slowly, wondering what was coming next.

"You're no stranger to her – that is the point. There is really no reason in the world why you shouldn't be dining in the Tower on the night of the twenty-sixth!"

She gasped her dismay.

"But…it is absolutely impossible!" she said.

"I expected you to say that," he answered with a smile.

"But suppose I dined there, what use could I be?" she broke in. "And don't you realise that, if Graham was suspected and it was known that I had spent the evening at the Tower, suspicion would attach to me?"

He inclined his head.

"You may credit me with having seen every aspect of the situation," he said quietly. "If you stay to dinner, that will be enough. Now listen, Diana – if I may be excused that liberty," he added, with a little bow.

She was not in a mood for ceremony, as her impatient gesture revealed.

"The Tower of London is one of our most picturesque anachronisms," he said. "There are certain practices and customs within the Tower which go back to mediaeval times, and amongst other things there is the practice of issuing a password of the night – that password I must have. On the morning of the twenty-sixth I shall know that it is one of four words: which one will not be decided till the very last minute."

She smiled at him.

"And who do you think will give me this piece of information?" she asked sarcastically.

"The Colonel," he said. "You will arrive in the Tower at seven o'clock, dressed for dinner."

"And I shall make my exit from the Tower at seven five," she said, with a twinkle in her eyes. "You don't know Lady Cynthia!"

"When you reach the Colonel's quarters," he went on, not noticing the interruption, "you will announce yourself to the servant, who will probably know you, and he in turn will announce you to the Colonel – "

"To Lady Cynthia," interrupted Diana.

"To the Colonel," insisted Tiger coolly. "Lady Cynthia will not be there. She will, in fact, be called away an hour before dinner to visit somebody. You need have no fear. Lady Cynthia Ruislip will not be in the Tower. But the Colonel will, and he will be astonished to see you, perhaps a little perturbed. You will tell him that somebody, who you thought was Lady Cynthia, telephoned you asking you to come to dinner. He will be astonished. You will hint that you have put off a very important engagement to come. What else can he do than ask you to stay to dinner and to share his meal? As to how you will get the password from him" – he shrugged his shoulders – "that is a matter for you. At ten o'clock you will ask him to see you home. Being something of a gallant, he will not refuse, especially as by this time Lady Cynthia will have notified him that she is not returning till midnight."

"You're very sure that all these things will happen," she said irritably.

"I am sure, because I shall make them happen," said Mr Trayne. "As you come out of the Tower a newspaper boy will approach you, and you will say 'No' if the word is one, "Thanks, no,' if the word is two, and so on. I think it will be one of four words: 'Newport,' 'Cardiff,' 'Monmouth,' or 'Bristol.' Memorise those, and when the Colonel has seen you home, what then? Detain him as long as you can, and after he has left you, go to bed and dream of" – he spread out his hands – "anything that is pleasant."

She walked to the window and frowned down into the street. Her heart was beating a little faster, at the very prospect of the adventure, and for the first time £50,000 did not look as enormous a sum as it had. Should she withdraw? She did not worry about Graham: he was not a factor in her life. In prison or out, Graham Hallowell was a responsibility and a nuisance. She wondered if he would divorce her if – Unfortunately he would not give her cause to initiate a suit.

"I don't like it very much – " she began, but something made her turn her head.

The room was empty. Tiger Trayne had chosen the psychological moment to leave her.

12

Fifty thousand pounds! She tried to flog up her enthusiasm for the project. Kishlastan had been generous, but he had always displayed evidence of weariness. He was a man without stamina, and now that he had found another and a more splendid vengeance on the people who had humiliated him, that source of income would dry up.

The right or wrong of the deed she was to further did not bother Diana. She was chiefly concerned with the safety or danger of it. She had a vague, uneasy consciousness of a crime called "high treason," for which the penalties were devastating. And yet – her part was such a small one, and, true to his principles, Trayne would so carefully guard her that, at the worst, detection was very unlikely.

On one thing she was determined. She would not see the book that Graham was reading nightly, nor allow herself to become acquainted with the details of the offence.

Dick Hallowell – what unconscious part was he to play? The attempt had been fixed for the night he was on guard, and in a way she felt a malicious pleasure that he would be implicated. Dick would be furious if he ever came to hear of her little talk with the Colonel. She had scotched the marriage, at any rate. Knowing something of his love for the regiment, she did not doubt that when he had to choose between this unknown girl with whom he had become infatuated, and his continuance with the battalion, he would choose for his career.

An idea struck her, and, sitting down at her table, she wrote a little note, addressed it to Lieutenant R. H. Longfellow, and dispatched it to the Tower by special messenger. Perhaps Bobbie would not come. But she had known him in his Eton days and he had always been very nice to her. She wanted badly to get the atmosphere of the Tower; to discover just how Dick Hallowell felt towards her; and when, at four o'clock that afternoon, Dombret came in and announced the young officer, she greeted him with a warmth that was rather staggering to Bobbie Longfellow.

He was not quite at his ease: she saw that at a glance, and it was not a hopeful sign. Bobbie was like a man caught in a furtive act, was stammering and apologetic for not having seen her for so long, and in the first breath announced that he had an engagement at five o'clock – an engagement which she guessed was wholly imaginary.

"You're a pig not to have come to see me before," she said. "How is Dick?"

Bobbie cleared his throat.

"Oh, pretty well," he said awkwardly.

"Did you tell him you were coming?"

There was a twinkle in her eye as she asked this question, and she was not surprised when he nodded.

"Thought I should, don't you know."

"I'm terribly curious, Bobbie: is Dick going to be married?"

Bobbie looked at the ceiling, and confessed that he had no information on the subject. It was not a good beginning, but gradually she worked him round to the subject of the Colonel, and she could more easily do this, for she had only met him on the previous night. And from the Colonel to Lady Cynthia was a step.

Bobbie thought she was "looking about the same."

"I wish Cynthia didn't loathe me so," said Diana with a sigh. "She used to be such a darling in the old days. Why, when she was a girl she was the gayest and most irresponsible member of the younger set in London – my mother told me that there were all sorts of scandals about her."

Bobbie gaped at this.

"There's nothing scandalous about her ladyship now," he said. "Quite the other way round, Diana. She's more like a jolly old iceberg than a human being. She simply freezes me."

"Did you ever mention my name to her?" asked Diana idly.

Bobbie was obviously uncomfortable.

"I forget," he said, a little more loudly than necessary... "Maybe... it is very likely."

And then Diana did a little intelligence work.

"Don't you think you could come to a little party of mine on the twenty-fifth?" she asked.

Bobbie made a rapid calculation.

"Sorry, I shall be taking that wretched guard on the twenty-fifth," he said. (Was there relief in his tone?) "Dick takes the guard on the twenty-sixth – we're rather short of officers; three of our fellows have been down with 'flu, and Joynson and Billingham are on leave. In fact, the Tower's the hardest job I've struck. There are more sentries in that wretched fortress than in a war camp."

Then, to her surprise, he asked: "Don't you like Hope Joyner?"

"Hope Joyner? Why, of course, Bobbie! I think she's perfectly sweet. I don't know her very well – but then, who does? She's rather a mysterious sort of person, isn't she?"

"I don't know," defended Bobbie stoutly. "She's no more mysterious than any other woman. I think she's a jolly nice girl."

"And she'll make Dick a good wife," she said quietly. "But he'll hate leaving the regiment."

Here was a challenge which, in his youthful enthusiasm, he was ready to accept.

"Why should he leave the regiment?" he demanded. "I mean, she isn't a chorus girl or – a – er – a person with a lot of scandal around her name."

"Of course he'll have to leave the regiment," she scoffed. "You know that as well as I, Bobbie – Hope Joyner hasn't a single string that attaches her to anybody we know, known or unknown."

Bobbie wriggled and grew red.

"If Hope Joyner isn't good enough for the Berwick Guards," he said doggedly, "then the Berwick Guards are not good enough for me! I'm not so horribly stuck on the Army that I'd stay in it a single day after Dick left. I've not heard anybody say a single word against Hope. Everybody thinks she's charming."

A little silence, and then Diana drawled: "Is that view shared by Lady Cynthia?" And to this question Bobbie had no reply.

Yet he could have made some interesting revelations, for Bobbie Longfellow had made this unknown girl's cause his own.

"I shouldn't be surprised" – he spoke haltingly, because he had to choose his words with the greatest care – "if quite a lot is known about Miss Joyner before there is any talk of an engagement."

Diana looked at him searchingly.

"How very mysterious!" she said. "And who is going to tell you?"

Bobbie could not give an answer here. He had arranged that night to call on Mr Hallett of Monk's Chase, though Mr Hallett was unaware of his intention.

"I shouldn't be surprised if we didn't find a whole lot," he said, lamely enough.

Diana could afford to be amused.

Bobbie walked downstairs a little puzzled as to the reason why Diana had sent for him, and more than ever confirmed in his belief that there was something very catlike about this charming lady. Diana's flat was on the first floor. He had reached the vestibule when a door at his elbow opened and a man came out, and walked briskly past him. Bobbie had a view of his face, and it was familiar, though for a moment he could not place him. He saw the porter in front of the door and beckoned to him.

"I know that gentleman. Who is he?"

The porter looked after the retreating figure.

"That's Mr Trayne, sir. He's a very well-known gentleman about town."

"Trayne?" Bobbie frowned. "Not Tiger Trayne? Not the chappie who – " He was going to say "owns all the gaming clubs," but thought it discreet to suppress this comment.

"Yes, sir, that's Mr Trayne." The porter was also a man of discretion, and remembered that Tiger Trayne was reputedly the owner of the block, and therefore his employer.

Of course! Bobbie remembered now a hectic night that had finished up in a superb West End mansion, where drinks were free, and a little crowd gathered about a green baize table throwing golden challenges to the goddess of fortune. Bobbie had lost money – not a great deal, for he had the cautiousness which is so often the characteristic of very rich men.

As he walked towards Piccadilly he tried to connect up in his mind certain ugly rumours that had circulated concerning Diana; rumours which, in truth and justice, had only the slenderest of foundations; for though she had once acted as an agent for Trayne in leading the feet of speculative youth to his green tables, it was not an experience that she had repeated.

Of Trayne he knew as much as the average man would hear. He was an adventurer, associated with a hundred shady transactions; a man who lived on the fringe of good society and had powerful friends in the most unexpected places.

Bobbie owned a little house in Curzon Street, and here he went to make his preparations, and to consult the memoranda that had been supplied by his agents. They were not promising. The beginnings of Hope Joyner were as obscure as ever. Whichever way the investigators turned, they came up against the brick wall represented by the firm of lawyers, none too reputable, who administered her estate and supplied her needs. A long and careful search through the registry had failed to discover a will under which she benefited.

By great cunning, Bobbie had discovered her age as twenty-three, and had concentrated upon the births on the 10th of June, 1901; but though Somerset House yielded him all its secrets, there was no Hope Joyner born on that day. It had seemed a simple matter to interview the blind Mr Hallett, but as the hour approached, something of Bobbie's confidence evaporated. He confided his doubts to the chief of his investigators, a saturnine private detective.

"I've no *locus standi*, old thing," he said, in despair. "The *modus operandi* is splendid, but the *locus standi* doesn't bear inspection."

"You can say that you're a friend of the family," suggested his assistant.

Bobbie shook his head.

"Which family?" he asked with staggering logic. "There isn't a family to be a friend of. If there was, I shouldn't go barging around the country looking for clues."

"Why not a friend of Miss Joyner's?" suggested the other, and Bobbie was annoyed.

"Haven't I explained to you a thousand times, my poor, simple fellow," he demanded in his exasperation, "that Miss Joyner's name is not to come into this business at all, and that nobody is even to guess that I'm interfering in her affairs? Have a heart!"

In the calm of the summer evening he reached Monk's Chase, descending from his car at the identical spot where, a week or so before, Hope Joyner had got down into the pouring rain. The lodge gates were open, the lodge itself apparently untenanted. Boldly he strode up the drive, and presently found himself pressing a bell at the forbidding main entrance. A few seconds later, the door opened noiselessly and a sedate footman presented himself.

"Mr Hallett, sir? Have you an appointment?"

Bobbie explained carefully that he had no appointment, but that he had come specially from London to interview the owner of Monk's Chase.

"I will see," said the footman, and ushering Bobbie into a small drawing room, he went out and was gone for some time. He came back with an apology.

"Mr Hallett is not feeling well," he said, "and he asked if you would be kind enough to write, telling him your business, sir. He has only just returned from Paris and is feeling very fatigued."

"Couldn't I see him for five minutes?"

And then, in desperation, he wrote a name upon a sheet of paper which he took from a small writing table, enclosed it in an envelope and said: "Give him this."

The footman shook his head.

"Mr Hallett is blind, sir. You probably did not know that."

Bobbie cursed his own stupidity under his breath.

"Hasn't he a secretary or somebody who can read it for him?"

"I'm afraid not, sir," said the footman.

Here, then, was another dead wall, and Bobbie found himself ushered through the big entrance and the door closed upon him, without having the least return for all his trouble.

In none too pleasant a temper he strode down the drive, through the lodge gates and on to the road; and here Fate took charge. Standing before the bonnet of his two seater was an aged man, examining with senile curiosity the somewhat daring mascot which ornamented the radiator. He was a very old man. He glared round.

"That young lady do look cold," he chuckled. "Never see anything like that down in these parts."

"I'll bet you don't!" said Bobbie. "How long have you lived around here?"

"Ninety-eight years," was the staggering reply.

"Moses!" gasped Bobbie. "You must be used to the neighbourhood by now."

"That I be," said the old gentleman complacently. "I remember Monk's Chase when old Lord Wilsome had it."

"And before Mr Hallett had it?" asked Bobbie, interested.

"Yes," said the old man contemptuously. "Why, it only seems yesterday all that fuss and bother there was when he runned away with a young lady and her feyther came down to shoot him. Highly connected she was."

Bobbie was all a-twitter with excitement.

"When was this?"

"Years and years ago there was a war on down in Africa. My grandson had his leg shot off and his pension to this day. A nice boy – "

Bobbie silenced the family reminiscences.

"Does anybody else know about this?"

"Here in the village?" said the old man contemptuously. "They knows nothing! They're all new people – why, there ain't nobody in this village except me an' the landlord of 'The Plough' that's been here more'n ten year!"

"How did you come to know about it?" asked Bobbie.

The old man grinned.

"My darter-in-law was a cook up at the Chase, and she got the rights of it."

So far as Bobbie could piece together, the unknown grand lady was also a married lady, married to a man much older than herself, from whom she had run away with the attractive Mr Hallett. She had been taken back by her indignant parents (the husband seemed strangely apathetic in the matter, not without reason it seemed, for he died very soon afterwards, and probably was little interested in the affairs of this world) and on her husband's death had married again.

"It was kept very quiet," said the ancient, " 'ushed up – that's the word, 'ushed up. According to what I have heard," the old man prattled on, "this lady what's-her-name married again."

"Mr Hallett?" suggested Bobbie.

The ancient shook his head.

"No, he never married. Appears they found out something about him; I never got the rights of it. But this Lady Cynthia – "

Bobbie put out his hand to the hot radiator for support, and such was his agitation that he did not yell at the burn.

"Lady Cynthia?" he gasped. "Oh, my great aunt!"

"Is she?" said the mistaken rustic. "I don't want to say nothing against your relations."

"Lady Cynthia – do you remember whom she married?"

The old man shook his head.

"I can't say. I don't know nobody that knew her. I only seen her once – a very tall, beautiful lady with a big green ring on her little finger. Worth hundreds of pounds, so people say."

Bobbie's head reeled. He knew that big emerald. How often had he seen Lady Cynthia Ruislip twisting it round and round her finger, whilst her cold eyes were appraising the virtues of flighty subalterns!

There was little more that the old man could tell him, and presently he ambled off, a little dazed himself by the munificence of the tip Bobbie put into his gnarled hand. Mr Longfellow sat down on the running board of his car, his head between his hands, an object of interest to local labourers homeward bound.

One thing was certain: he must see Mr Hallett that night.

He walked along the road till he came to the picturesque village, and the first thing he saw was an inn sign that reminded him of something the old man had said. The landlord was one of the men who knew the story of Mr Hallett's great adventure. Going into the parlour, which was untenanted, he saw behind the counter an elderly man polishing a glass, and him Bobbie greeted. He was not so loquacious, however, as the ancient. It was some time before Bobbie could get him to speak.

"I suppose you've been talking to Gammer Holland? That old gentleman babbles like a woman! I know very little about the matter, and I don't care to talk scandal about my neighbours, especially a gentleman like Mr Hallett, who's – well, not a customer, but we've done business together."

"Do you know the lady in the case?"

The landlord shook his head.

"No, sir, I never inquired. I've got an idea…however, my ideas are not evidence, are they? I know she married an officer in the Guards some time after, but that's about the extent of my knowledge."

Seemingly this was so, for Bobbie could get no further information from him.

He lingered for an hour at the inn, the landlord supplying him with a passable dinner, and as soon as it got dark he went out on a reconnaissance. He was anxious to get back to the Tower by midnight, for he had not left his name in the leave book and there was just a chance that the watchman whose duty it was to admit officers between midnight and three o'clock in the morning, might not be available.

It was still dusk when he wandered up towards the house, not directly, as he had gone before, but following a path which brought him without fear of observation to a point opposite the west wing of the building. By the time he reached here it was dark enough for his purpose, and making a cautious way across the broad lawn, he reached the wing and went slowly along the front, passing – though he was not aware of the fact – the door through which Hope Joyner had made her entrance to Monk's Chase.

He had to pass the entrance, and here was a semicircle of noisy gravel; he was hesitating whether he should follow the grass when he saw the lights of a motorcar twinkling through the trees at the far end of the drive. He looked around for a place of concealment: there was only one – a niche formed by the outspread portico, and he squeezed himself between wall and pillar, hoping that the lights of the car would not reveal him. Evidently they did not, for the driver stopped before the door, and descending, knocked.

"He won't be a minute," said a low voice, and the chauffeur went back to his seat.

Bobbie waited, his heart beating a little faster. If the "he" referred to was Mr Hallett, what should he do? Should he jump out of his place of concealment, seize him conventionally by the arm and say: "I've got a few words to say to you"? Or –

He had no time to make up his mind. A brisk step sounded on the flagstones. Mr Hallett passed to the door of the car, paused for a second to light a cigarette, and, peeping forth, Bobbie Longfellow saw his strong face…

He felt it was not the moment to make his presence known.

13

Graham Hallowell had many unpleasant moments; moments of doubt, anxiety and sheer fretfulness. His loneliness gave him far too much time to think. Once he called up Diana and urged her to come down to him. But she had an important engagement of some kind. He thought she was lying, but for once did her an injustice.

Mawsey, the gardener, had gone, and another and younger man had taken his place, and carried out his duties with the same punctilious care as his predecessor.

By this time Graham knew the plan by heart; and the better acquainted he was with it and the simpler it seemed, the more uneasy he became; for this narrative of Trayne's was confident to a point of madness. It said nothing as to how the jewels were to be taken. Graham's part was simple enough. But he knew more than a little of the Tower routine and the extraordinary safeguards which surrounded the regalia. As his uneasiness increased, he resolved to see at first hand just what difficulties there were to be overcome.

He chose a Saturday, which was a public half-holiday, when he knew that the Tower would be crowded with visitors, and, joining the queue at the ticket office, he gained the little green pasteboard that admitted him to the Jewel House and followed the holidaymakers through the first guarding arch, along the curtain wall, till he came to the Bloody Tower.

A warder would have headed him off, because visitors are expected to follow a prescribed route, but allowed him to pass when he showed the green ticket. Again he had to wait, all the time in fear lest he should be observed by somebody who knew him. He saw the officer of the guard, a stranger to him, and breathed a sigh of relief. Presently he was mounting the steps of the Wakefield Tower, where the jewels are housed.

The outer door was of stout oak, backed, he guessed, with steel. It was when he reached the landing where was the door admitting to the Jewel House that he had his first shock. The door of the regalia chamber consisted of two steel leaves. They were strongroom doors, four inches thick. In the centre of the room was a steel cage, the sides of which were thick plate glass. Looking down into the interior he saw a small air pressure gauge, which told its own story. The emergency shutters he could detect. At the first hint of danger, a warder, told off specially for the duty, would touch the secret lever and the shutters would fall with a crash.

By night either they or another set would slowly descend and lock automatically. He could see the big steel grip which fastened them. The jewels he hardly saw. The baleful glare of the Black Prince's ruby, the glittering splendours of the African diamonds, none of these interested him.

He was curious to discover whether it was possible to detect the electric alarm, which, at the first attempt to move shutter or splinter glass, would sound alarm bells in every part of the Tower. The connections were invisible, but they were there nevertheless. He made a slow circuit with the crowd, and was glad when he came out into the open air.

Alongside the Wakefield Tower was a big, ugly guardroom of red brick, the most hideous anachronism that the Tower contained.

Finding a disengaged warder, he chartered him to show him the interior of the little church – "the saddest spot in Christendom." But it was not the coats of arms in the tessellated pavement above the bodies of the dead and the great, or the unmarked graves of the Pretender's victims, that held him.

"…Yes, sir, there's an extra guard on the Jewel House at night; in fact there are two."

"I suppose they're pretty well guarded?" suggested Graham.

"Guarded?" The warder laughed. "I should say so! Sometimes those darned alarm wires get short-circuited in the night, and the whole of the Tower stands under arms!"

A promising prospect, thought Graham gloomily, as he left the grim fortress behind him. He had intended returning to Cobham, but he felt that he must see Diana and took his chance of finding her in. It did not improve his temper to find Colley Warrington installed in the drawing room, for Colley, in his moments of relaxation, adopted an attitude which was almost proprietorial. He might have been the owner of the flat, thought Graham, from the cool nod of half welcome he gave the new arrival.

"Hullo, Graham! Rusticating, they tell me?"

"Is Diana here?" asked the other shortly.

"She's here, yes. We're going on to tea at the Canton."

"You'd better find another companion: I want a long talk with her."

Colley's insolent stare was maddening.

"What a masterful fellow he is!" he said in mock admiration. "Unfortunately, Diana has an engagement – a business engagement."

"Then she can break it." In his exasperation he was near to betraying his relationship. Fortunately, Diana came in at that moment, and a glance at his face told her that something was wrong.

"I want a private talk with you, Diana. Colley tells me he's taking you out to tea; is it possible for you to put off that engagement?"

She glanced at Colley.

"I think so," she said, to the man's amazement.

"My dear Diana – " he began.

She shook her head.

"I'm sorry, Colley, but I think this is rather important. If you don't mind, I will join you at the hotel at six o'clock."

When Diana spoke in that tone of voice it was useless to argue, and Mr Colley Warrington, faithful to his traditional methods, smiled and made the best effort possible to conceal his chagrin.

She walked with him to the door, and when they were in the passage outside he said in a low voice: "I don't think it will be wise to take friend Graham into your confidence – about the matter we discussed this afternoon."

To this she made no reply. Closing the door upon him, she came back quickly to Graham.

"What has happened?" she asked.

He was looking at her through narrowed lids.

"What did that fellow have to tell you that couldn't be said here?" he demanded. He was not a jealous man, but now his nerves were on edge.

"He asked me to marry him this afternoon," she said calmly, "and his last words were a request that I should not take you into my confidence and tell you of that interesting proposal. Colley is slimy, but he's useful. Now, what is it?"

He was pacing up and down the carpet, his hands in his pockets.

"Trayne is mad – as mad as a March hare. I've been to the Tower to look over the Jewel House. It is easier to rob the Bank of England!"

In a few words he told her the precautions that had been taken against robbery.

"The old fool is thinking two hundred years wrong," he said. "The Jewel House is a safe. The cleverest cracksman in the world, English or American, could not open the steel doors, and if he did, he'd have twice the trouble to get inside the cage. There are alarm bells everywhere, and all the leads are concealed, probably in the wall. The thing is humanly impossible."

She bit her lip thoughtfully.

"It doesn't sound like Trayne to tackle the impossible. I was talking with Colley about him this afternoon, and Colley says he's the cleverest man in the world at his game."

She looked at him long and earnestly.

"Your part, Graham – do you think it is dangerous?"

He shook his head.

It is dangerous, but possible. In fact, I think that is the most ingenious section of the scheme. I know the military routine thoroughly – I was at Sandhurst, remember, and for two years in the

Westshires. No, I'm not worried about that: my nerves are good enough and strong enough. It's the actual robbery that's hitting me. Trayne has allowed only a quarter of an hour for it. It will take him a quarter of an hour to get through the oak door, and he'd be lucky if he did it in the time. I've had talks with all sorts of expert burglars in Dartmoor – Vrenehy, who smashed the Southern Bank, told me that the cleverest of burglars couldn't get through a modern safe under three hours. They want a weekend to do the job thoroughly, and even then they must have freedom to move about, electric plugs – oh, the thing is impossible! Absolutely impossible, Diana. I must see Trayne."

She nodded at this.

"He is going down to Cobham tomorrow night," she said. "I had a note from him, asking me to be there. We must have this thing out, Graham. I'm worried sick about it all."

She watched him as he lit a cigarette and threw the stalk with unerring aim halfway across the room into the fireplace. There was the making of a good man in Graham. He hadn't grown straight; there had been some little obstacles in the way of his mental and spiritual development, something that had thrown him out of the true. She had loved him once, tempestuously, insanely – she had never quite disliked him. In this moment of his dilemma and stress she felt something of the old affection returning. It was not an unpleasant sensation.

"We shall have to worry this out tomorrow night, Graham – and we'll worry it together," she said.

He detected instantly the change in her tone, and looked at her quickly. Perhaps he, too, saw something more in her than an irksome tie, for the strained face creased in a little smile: it was the first smile that she had seen since his release from prison.

"Perhaps it's not worth while getting rattled about," he said. "Old man Trayne isn't exactly a fool. He knows the difficulties as well as you or I."

"Does the book tell you?" she asked. "I mean, does it tell you how the Wakefield Tower is to be broken into?"

He shook his head.

"He passes over that very airily," he said, and smiled again. Then suddenly he held out his hand. "I'm glad I came to see you, Diana. I don't know whether it's the atmosphere of the room or your own peculiar qualities, but I feel more cheery about things now."

He left her by no means cheery; to her other troubles was added another, which until that afternoon had not existed – anxiety for his safety.

14

Dick Hallowell did not often make a call upon his Colonel's wife, and Lady Cynthia was obviously surprised when he was announced. She sat on the edge of a low settee, her tea table before her, a straight-backed, slim creature, with delicately moulded features, and lips a trifle too thin to be beautiful. Bobbie had summed up Lady Cynthia Ruislip in one sentence: "When you see her you think she's thirty: when you hear her you know she's a hundred," he had said unkindly. All the charm and freshness of a girl, all the acid wisdom of a woman, were combined in this languid lady.

"This is a very fine honour, Dick," she drawled. "You are the first to arrive. Shall I ring for tea?"

"Pray don't. I hoped to see you before the others came," he said.

It was Lady Cynthia's "afternoon": a period of ordeal for young subalterns, for her ladyship had remarkable sources of information, and many a youth had stood aghast whilst she narrated some adventure of his which he hoped had ended when he had tipped an irate policeman, or placated the ruffled commissionaire charged with escorting him from a night club in which he had made himself objectionable.

"Sit down. You don't want tea – you want to talk – about Miss Joyner, of course," said Lady Cynthia precisely.

In spite of himself, Dick Hallowell felt the blood mounting to his face.

"Yes, it is about Miss Joyner. I have asked her to come up to dinner in my rooms tomorrow, and I was wondering whether I could persuade you to act as hostess, Lady Cynthia?"

Her bright blue eyes stared at him unwinkingly. There was a pause, and then: "Why, of course, I shall be delighted. It is Miss Hope Joyner, the gel who lives at Devonshire House – everybody is talking about her: they say she is immensely pretty."

"She is immensely nice, too," said Dick emphatically.

There was an almost imperceptible lift of the shoulder, he saw, and was prepared for what was to come.

"She is one of the Yorkshire Joyners, isn't she? Or is it Warwickshire – I knew a very good family there many years ago."

"I have no knowledge of her family," said Dick.

Her ladyship's eyebrows rose inquiringly.

"Surely not? You don't mean – ?" She left him to reply.

"I mean, I don't know who her people are, and I don't think she does either. She is a lady and she's very charming. I am hoping that you will give her a welcome to the regiment, Lady Cynthia."

She was looking down at the tea table now, and when he finished she sighed.

"It is very difficult, isn't it? You realise, of course, Dick, how awfully careful one has to be – about the women our people marry? I hope you will be awfully happy, whether you stay – "

"Please don't make up your mind whether I'm staying or not, if you mean whether I'm staying in the regiment, Lady Cynthia," he said, with all the patience he could summon. "Won't you see her first?"

"Of course," she answered at once. "Perhaps you haven't asked her – about her family, I mean?"

"Oh, yes, I've asked her," said Dick quietly, as he rose to go. "I may expect you, then, at eight?"

She held out her jewelled hand and smiled up at him.

"I do hope everything will be all right, Dick," she almost cooed. "It would be such a dreadful loss to the regiment if you had to go."

He literally ran into Bobbie as he was leaving the Colonel's quarters.

"Going in for my weekly sacrifice," said Bobbie, without cheer. "How's the old lady?"

"The old lady's alone," said Dick savagely, "and I wish you joy of her."

"Dear me!" said Bobbie mildly, and allowed himself to be announced.

"The very man I wanted to see!"

He had never known her ladyship so cheerful or enthusiastic. Conscience-stricken, he ran over such exploits as he had to his week's discredit, but could find no excuse for so much as a quake.

"I've just been talking to Dick Hallowell. You're a great friend of his, aren't you?"

"Pretty great!" said Bobbie cautiously, not quite certain to what extent he might be called to account, if he made the admission more definite.

"Who is this wretched Joyner girl?"

"A very nice lady," said Bobbie lamely.

"Is he engaged?"

Bobbie shook his head.

"But he will be?"

Bobbie nodded.

"Can't you persuade him?"

"Look here, Lady Cynthia," Bobbie was stung to reply, and at the peremptory character of his voice she looked at him open-mouthed, "I thought it was only a woman with a past you didn't want in the regiment?"

She smiled slowly.

"That's the kind we want," she said good humouredly. "A past you can trace for a hundred years or so."

"Not twenty or thirty years or so?" asked Bobbie, and instantly she brought her eyes to his. "I mean, would you consider" – his mouth was dry; it was only by an effort of will that he could get his tongue to move, he was in such awe of this beautiful woman – "would a lady be considered eligible for the – regiment – if she had – a disgraceful affair – twenty-five years ago, or maybe twenty-six?" he asked jerkily.

There was speculation in the regiment as to whether Lady Cynthia's colour was natural, whether the pink in her face owed something to artifice. He could have set all doubts at rest, for all of a sudden her face was very white.

"I don't quite follow you, Mr Longfellow."

"I'm merely asking," he went on doggedly: "does time wipe out that sort of thing, or is it like a motor licence where you can renew the clean sheet every three years? Or is it one of those jolly old Book of Judgment leaves that stay put?"

" 'Stay put' is rather foreign to me," she said. "Of whom are you speaking? Who had some disgraceful episode in her life – twenty-five years ago?"

"I didn't say 'her.' " Bobby could have howled with joy at his own brilliance.

"You were talking about a woman," she countered quickly.

"I was talking about nobody," said Bobbie mendaciously. "I merely asked whether that kind of thing is – retrospective?"

She drew a long breath; the colour was coming slowly back to her cheeks.

"Riddles make my head ache." And when at that moment the adjutant and Bobbie's company commander came in, she made no attempt to hide her relief.

"Got you, old lady!"

Bobbie whistled as he strode out on to the square, and was so preoccupied that he almost forgot to return the salutes which greeted him as his long legs carried him down past the guardhouse under the eight-hundred-year-old portcullis of the Bloody Tower.

The sergeant of the gate guard was standing at the end of the bridge over the moat, watching the drilling of defaulters. He stiffened to attention as his officer approached, and, remembering something, Bobbie stopped and asked a question.

"Yes, sir," said the sergeant, "Sir Richard has just gone out."

Sprinting, Bobbie overtook his friend as he was stepping into a taxi.

"I'm going west, too," said Bobbie, as he dropped into the cab.

He glanced at Dick Hallowell's clouded face and chuckled.

"Cynthia was certainly in form this afternoon. She nearly got me rattled, too. I gathered, from your wild and ferocious expression when you barged into me, that you'd been discussing Hope Joyner with her ladyship?"

Dick nodded.

"She seems to have determined that I shall leave the regiment," he said bitterly. "And really, I don't see how I can fight her in view of everything. The Colonel's been very decent about Graham, and I shall have to give way on this question. I don't really mind leaving the Army, though it breaks a family tradition. What makes me mad is the implied slight on Hope."

Then Bobbie remembered something.

"Talking of Graham, he was in the Tower this afternoon."

Dick looked at him in astonishment.

"The devil he was! Who told you?"

"My servant saw him, lining up like a tripper outside the Jewel House."

Dick's face was troubled.

"Graham isn't the sort of bird who finds any pleasure in crowds, and a half-holiday is the last day in the world I should have expected him to go sightseeing. Besides, he knows the Tower almost as well as I. That's queer."

"I don't think it is as queer as you think," said Bobbie. "This is the day of all days he would come to the Tower if he came at all, when there are so many people about that he would pass unnoticed in the crowd."

Dick shook his head.

"Why should he wish to pass unnoticed?" he asked. "Jewel House? I've never known Graham to take a patriotic interest in the regalia."

The thought of his brother occupied his mind until they were passing through Trafalgar Square, when Bobbie said, apropos of nothing: "I'd like you to promise me something – don't resign your commission, or even tell the Colonel or any of the other fellows that you intend resigning, until you have talked this out with me."

Dick smiled.

"There is only one person in the world with whom I can talk this out, Bobbie," he said, "and I'm seeing her in five minutes' time."

He was dreading the interview as he passed into the beautiful vestibule of Devonshire House. That he was to hurt her by the implied and remote reflection upon her birth, was hateful to him; and she must have read aright the glumness of his face as she came across the panelled hall to greet him, for of a sudden her smile faded.

Then suddenly, without warning, he took her by the shoulders and, stooping, kissed her. He had never kissed her before, and he felt her tremble under his hands. No word was spoken, no whispered declaration or shy response. With his arm about her shoulder, they walked back to her drawing room, and he closed the door...

For a second they stood looking at one another gravely, searchingly.

"I never dreamt I should do that," he said simply. "It just – happened."

And then, without waiting for her answer: "I saw Lady Cynthia Ruislip – my Colonel's wife – this afternoon – "

"And she doesn't approve of me," she said quickly. "She has never approved because – because I am a nobody. Isn't that so, Dick?"

He nodded. It was not a moment for polite interpretation.

"Somebody has told you?" he asked.

She shook her head.

"No, I've known it for a long time – I just felt it. Does that mean you would have to leave the regiment?"

"I shall leave the Army, anyway – " he began.

"You're not telling me the truth; you're leaving because they don't want me. And I'm not going to let you do it."

Her voice was very steady and quiet; he had never seen her calmer or more serene; her very attitude inhibited the protest which rose to his lips.

"Not yet, at any rate. You must know who I am, Dick – the best or the worst. I think Lady Cynthia is right – more right than if she were objecting to the daughter of a chimney sweep coming into the regiment."

"I shall leave the Army," he said doggedly, but she shook her head with a smile.

"You don't know what an effort it requires to say 'no' to that, Dick," she said, her wonderful eyes on his. "Everything that is in me says 'Yes' so loudly that I almost wonder you do not hear it!"

"But, Hope, I want you!" Her hands were imprisoned in his. "I can't let you go – nothing on God's earth will make me give you up! I love you! All my life revolves round you."

When she spoke it was slowly, haltingly: "There will be no – giving up, Dick. I couldn't, I couldn't – "

In another instant she was in his arms, his cheek against her fragrant head, and he felt the throb and quiver of the body he held tightly against his.

When Mr Trayne took a journey he moved swiftly and followed a route that could not be anticipated by the shrewdest of detectives. His car was as fast as any on the road, could outdistance any pursuers, and the telephone was useless if employed by the police to warn outlying stations that he might be passing, so that he could be trailed to his destination. For he followed strange ways, and came to Cobham in the dusk via Reading. Diana had already arrived, and was sipping a cup of indifferent coffee that the new cook had made for her, when he came into the pretty little sitting room and, with a glance round to make sure that the windows were shuttered and curtained, threw his hat on the sofa and sat down.

"Is the tailor satisfactory?" he asked.

"Yes," said Graham shortly; "he fitted me today."

"Good!" He smiled quizzically into Diana's serious face. "You're scared stiff," he said, "and I know why. Graham has told you of the scheme?"

"Yes, he's told me all he knows," she said significantly.

"Exactly." He laughed softly, as at a private jest.

"It's the bit he hasn't told you, and the bit he doesn't know, which has put your nerves on edge?"

"Trayne, this thing is absolutely impossible!" It was Graham who broke impatiently into the conversation. "I've been to the Tower to see the Jewel House, and – it's impossible! It's the maddest scheme that was ever devised. Why, it would take you hours to get through the safe door. I suppose you know there are strongroom doors across the entrance of the room? I suppose you realise that every bar and every shutter has an electrical connection? The moment you attempted to move or cut anything, bells would ring in every part of the infernal place." He ended a little breathlessly.

Trayne was not annoyed, as he had expected, but he was obviously amused.

"I know you went to the Tower; I can tell you the number of the ticket you took, the name of the warder who showed you round the church, what you said to him, and all that he said to you. Impossible, is it?" His keen eyes scrutinised the younger man's face. "Do you imagine," he said, slowly and emphatically, "that I'm such a congenital idiot that I'd tackle a job like this if it was – impossible? Do you imagine that I am not also aware of the fact that there are strongroom doors across the entrance, that there are alarm signals to every bar and every plate – or do you think that you are giving me information?"

The sarcasm in his tone irritated Graham.

"Of course, I expected you had reconnoitred the ground, but even then – "

"Even then, you still think it's impossible? How long do you imagine I've been working on this job?"

It was Diana who answered.

"Kishlastan has been in the country six months – "

"Kishlastan!" he said contemptuously. "Kishlastan is merely the receiver I've been waiting for for ten years. Ten? It was twelve years ago when I first made my plans to relieve the Governor of the Tower of this responsibility. And for twelve years the regalia has been a hobby of mine. I know it so well that I could draw from memory the ivory sceptre, the coronation spoon, every crown, every diadem. I could reproduce the cutting of the big diamonds, could tell you within a millimetre the size of the Black Prince's ruby.

He stopped, laughed shortly and, biting off the end of a cigar, lit it.

"And I could tell you something more. I'm one of the few men outside the officials who can work the shutters. I know every alarm connection – those two steel doors at the entrance are old friends of mine. Listen!"

He lowered his voice and, his elbows on the table, leaned over towards Graham Hallowell.

"When the custodian of the regalia wants to take out a crown or a sceptre, does he have to cut through the iron doors? Does he alarm the Tower? Does he have to use a 'gas-lamp' on the bars?"

"Of course he doesn't," said Graham impatiently. "He takes his keys – "

"Exactly; he takes his keys, he turns his levers, and in five minutes he lifts out whatever article or articles he requires. And that is exactly what I shall do!"

He sat pulling at his cigar in a contemplative silence, his eyes fixed on the wall. They did not interrupt his meditations, and after a while he spoke.

"Have you explored your domain?" he asked.

For the moment Graham thought he was talking metaphorically.

"The grounds, I mean."

"Why, yes. I've walked around – why?"

"Have you seen the stone tower in the plantation?"

The very existence of the stone building had passed out of Graham's mind.

"The granary? Yes."

Trayne chuckled.

"Granary! That is rather good! We haven't disturbed you at nights?"

Graham looked at him in astonishment.

"Disturbed me? Have you been here?"

The man nodded.

"Every other night. Half a dozen of us. Would you like to inspect the 'granary'?"

He rose as he put the question.

"One moment, Mr Trayne. There is something I'd like to ask you," said Diana. "Nobody understands better than you what the consequences might be if we are detected. And yet everybody seems to be in your secret – Graham, I, the men you are employing – "

He interrupted with a laugh.

"It is going to be a little difficult to prove, isn't it?" he asked coolly. "And when everything is over, what does it matter who squeals? The thing will be so big, it will be more like a war than a crime. It doesn't matter who started the war, once it is fairly going; and it doesn't matter who takes these jewels – once they're gone. It wouldn't matter much if he walked down Regent Street with a placard on his back announcing the fact. The question of his punishment is a small matter compared with recovering the stolen property. Besides, Kishlastan is in this, as you know, and they couldn't keep him out of it, not if they tried." Then, peremptorily: "Come along!"

They followed him through the garden and along the rough path that led into the plantation. Once he turned to warn them not to use lights.

"If you can't see me, you'd better touch my shoulder, Miss Martyn, and Hallowell had better hold on to yours. There is nothing to trip you up."

At last the tower loomed out of the darkness before them, and without hesitation he walked to the little door and the girl heard the soft snap of the lock. There was no sign of light inside when the door opened noiselessly. He warned them to lower their heads and ushered the two into a small vaulted chamber, and closed the door after him. There was a click and a flood of light, blinding after the darkness, illuminated the interior.

They were in a small stone lobby, from which led a circular staircase. There was something familiar to Graham in this entrance.

The first thing he noticed was that, although the tower was square outside, it was circular within. He was half way up the broad stairs when, with a gasp, he realised the significance and purpose of the "granary," and any doubt he might have had was set at rest when they came to the landing, for confronting them was a pair of steel strongroom doors.

Tiger Trayne took a key from his waistcoat pocket, unlocked them, and they swung heavily inward. Again a flood of light, and Diana looked open-mouthed at the sight which met her eyes. In the centre of a circular chamber was a large glass and steel cage, in which was symmetrically deposited a number of wooden blocks and rods. The interior of the cage was brightly illuminated, and Graham recognised the wooden contents. That square box was the Crown of Edward, that long rod the diamond sceptre – the cage contained wooden Crown jewels, each in its proper place.

"Now I will show you," said Trayne's voice, and as he spoke there came a hiss of sound and heavy steel shutters came down inside the glass and hid the interior from view. "Watch!"

They could not see what he was doing, but the shutters were rising again. He walked to one of the faces of the cage, and Graham watched, fascinated; saw him reach into the interior and lift out the block of wood.

"But the alarm bells?" he said huskily.

"They won't ring, because they can't ring," was the cool reply. "I confess they were one of the big difficulties. It took me two years' hard thinking and the assistance of a clever Swedish electrician to discover how the alarms were to be put out of action. But that difficulty has been overcome. You need not worry – you do your part of the work, and the rest will be easy. I want to see you tomorrow night and every night until the twenty-second. You will be dressed for the part."

"Suppose there is a hitch?"

"There will be no hitch." Trayne almost snapped the words as he turned the key in the lock of the great door.

Walking before him into the plantation, Graham Hallowell's head was in a whirl; but Diana's brain was like ice. She could see the scheme as Tiger Trayne saw it, could see success at the end; only –

"How long will Graham be away?"

"Three months at the most," said Trayne, lowering his voice as they went through the plantation and across the lawn to the house.

"Do you think they may suspect him?"

"Does it matter whom they suspect?" asked the Tiger impatiently.

15

If the Prince of Kishlastan was mad, there were certain practical aspects of his madness. For example, he had enormous balances on deposit in various countries. The immense sum he drew to pay Trayne came from America, and it was in dollar currency that he was to receive his reward.

On the eve of his departure for Kishlastan, His Excellency had two interviews; the first, without concealment, with Colley Warrington; the second, that none saw, with Trayne. This probably took place in a closed car circling the park – a favourite method of the Tiger's, and one which reduced the possibility of being overlooked and overheard to a minimum. Colley's took place at the hotel, and that slippery man of affairs had a cheerful account to give of his interview with Captain Eli Boss.

"He's going down river tomorrow night. I have fixed everything with him, and the matter is settled."

"Did you have the furniture taken on board?" asked Riki. "She must be surrounded by luxury – "

Colley shook his head.

"It was impossible," he said. "The ship is being watched by the Customs officers and probably by – " He was going to say "the police," but thought it less alarming to change the word to "authorities." "A boatload of swagger furniture going on board would have aroused suspicion. There's bound to be a kick the moment they hear of her disappearance. Anyway – we needn't advertise the fact that she is going by the *Pretty Anne*."

"Have you arranged with her?"

Colley nodded.

"Yes, she's dining with me on the night of the twenty-fourth. I've hinted to her that I know something about her parentage. In fact, I have half promised that I will clear up that little mystery. And of course she bit. We're dining in a little restaurant off Villiers Street. And I told her to wear her day clothes because I might have to take her to some place where evening dress would make her a little too conspicuous. She jumped at that too. It is going to be easy."

"People will know you dined with her." The Prince was biting his nails thoughtfully.

Colley shook his head with a laugh.

"That is the one thing she will not tell. I emphasised that very strongly; told her that I myself was breaking my word, and that nobody must know I was her informant. I was scared to death she would tell Hallowell, but I extracted a promise of secrecy from her, and she's the kind of girl who won't go back on her word."

Riki paced up and down the apartment, his thin brown hands clasped behind him, a vacant look in his dark eyes.

"This man Eli Boss – it sounds almost Indian – he is reliable?"

There was a peculiar expression in his face when he asked this question. It was as though he was thinking of Eli's trustworthiness in some other direction.

"Absolutely reliable, I should think, if you pay him well enough," said Colley, and the ghost of a smile showed in his face. "I don't think he's too friendly with friend Trayne, and part of the satisfaction he's getting is due to the illusion that he's double-crossing the old man. He promised to ship a girl to look after Miss Joyner."

"That is unnecessary if you are going," interrupted the rajah quickly. "I do not wish that a woman should be with her – one of my own women, yes, but I have none here."

"So I thought. Though it would be all the better if there was a – an Indian woman who could attend to her. I am not looking forward to the trip. One of the sons of the captain is bringing the launch to London, by the way."

He took a paper from his pocket and handed it to his master.

"Here is the approximate time table. We reach the rendezvous on the Indian coast within forty-eight hours of that day." He pointed to the date. "I have arranged the signals and the landing should be a simple matter."

They spent the next hour discussing details of the plan, and Colley left the hotel with the first part of his payment.

Rikisivi was mad; he was quite satisfied on that point; he was madder than anybody he had ever met, though he had his lucid intervals. Yet, not for one moment did Colley Warrington regret the unspeakable outrage he contemplated. The very magnitude of it was a salve to what was left of his conscience. If he wished anything, it was that the Prince's other enterprise had been postponed for a month or two. He knew none of the details, except that Trayne was in it and that some big iniquity was planned – another girl perhaps… If he had had an idea that Graham Hallowell was to accompany him to India, he might have viewed his forthcoming trip with even greater abhorrence than in fact he did.

On his way home he called in at the Mousetrap Club, wondering whether, if he saw Trayne, he would get any hint as to the nature of the second operation. The Tiger was in the beautiful little writing room, a cup of coffee by his side, a half-smoked cigar in its saucer, and with his glasses perched on his nose he was writing a letter. He glanced round as the door opened, for he was the only occupant of the room, and welcomed Colley with a growl.

"I've just been up to see our mutual friend."

Colley helped himself to a cigar from the case which lay at the Tiger's elbow.

"That is the worst news I've had for years," said Trayne, folding his glasses deliberately and as deliberately turning the sheet of paper he was writing on upside down so that it could not be read.

Mr Warrington was amused in his bored way – the Tiger's oblique jests had a salty flavour.

"I don't get you," he said as he snicked off the end and lit the cigar before he dropped into the most comfortable chair in the room.

"I didn't know we had any mutual friends. Who was this unfortunate person?" asked Trayne, his shaggy eyebrows straightening in a frown.

"Shall we call him the gentleman from India?"

"Riki? Did you teach him piquet?" There was a sting in the question. It was his skill in the game of piquet which had largely brought about Colley Warrington's social obfuscation.

Colley laughed. He was unstingable.

"You know him, don't you? He told me you were doing a job for him. Can I come into it, on the side?"

Trayne took the stub of his cigar from his saucer and relit it.

"Yes – on the outside. To tell you the truth, Colley, he's tired of seeing you and he asked me to find a couple of men to put you out! But offal-hunting was never a hobby of mine."

Still Colley was not annoyed.

"I've often wondered," he said lazily, "why you and I are not better friends?"

Tiger Trayne laughed.

"Wonder no more," he answered promptly. "I don't like you and I don't trust you. They are two pretty good reasons, aren't they?"

"I admire frankness, even in you," smiled Colley. "What do you really object to in me?"

Trayne answered instantly. He used a word which of all words was most offensive to Colley Warrington, and this time the Tiger drew blood, for two pink spots appeared in the sallow face.

"That's a word I don't like," he snarled.

"I guessed you wouldn't. If I'd used it to almost the lowest thief I know, he'd have pulled a gun on me – and rightly. But I don't know any other word that better fits a man who has exploited women so shamelessly as you, Warrington. And now, if you don't mind, I'll finish my letter."

Colley Warrington left the Mousetrap Club trembling with rage – not for the first time in his life had the Tiger touched one of his few raw spots. His nimble mind sought round for a way by which he could hurt this criminal; and yet, behind his desire for vengeance, was a wholesome fear of the complicated organisation which Tiger Trayne controlled.

Yet he might have spared himself the wear and the labour of thinking out schemes of vengeance. It was fated that he and Tiger Trayne were never to meet again.

16

The twenty-fourth dawned on the Tower greyly. A thin white mist covered the waters; overhead the skies were heavy and tearful. Towards twelve o'clock the drizzle turned into a downpour, that did not vary in intensity throughout the rest of the afternoon.

On such days as these the Tower is a desolation, the drill square empty, visitors very rare indeed. Sentries stand snug in their boxes, the warders in their long cloaks disappear into such kiosks or doorways as give them shelter.

It was raining heavily enough when Dick Hallowell marched his guard off the square and lined them before the red guardhouse. He made his rounds with Bobbie, whom he was relieving, took over the wharf and the "spur" guards, and was glad when Bobbie's men, marched away and he was free to find the shelter of his room.

They had a few minutes' chat before the guard moved off.

"I wish you'd go along and see Hope today," he said, "and tell her why I cancelled the dinner in my room."

"Lady Cynthia is furious with you; I suppose you know that?"

"I thought she would be, but that doesn't worry me at all. Why she should be furious, heaven knows. Did she tell you she was angry?"

Bobbie shook his head.

"She told Davenport; Cynthia said she'd put off an engagement especially to meet your wretched young woman – those were her words – and that you'd left her flat!"

Dick smiled faintly.

"She'd hardly be so slangy! But it doesn't really matter about Lady Cynthia. See Hope. I wrote her a letter and I think she understands, but I'd rather you had a talk with her."

Soon after the old guard marched off, and Dick faced a twenty-four hour duty which was not entirely free from interest, but a long way from being free from boredom.

Lady Cynthia was not in her most amiable mood that day, and if her husband had had the slightest excuse for absenting himself he would have made his escape. Unfortunately, duty kept him in the Tower and he had perforce to sit and suffer.

"Very thoughtless, I'm sure, my dear," he murmured for the *n*th time. "But Dick is rather touchy on the question of his girl."

"Touchy!" she scoffed. "He's impertinent! And the contagion seems to have spread to that stupid fool Longfellow. He not only asked me to go to dinner with him, but he wrote me a note confirming the invitation, and then at the last minute 'the dinner is cancelled, because, I presume, this young person funked it!"

"Which young person?" asked the Colonel, who was thinking of something else.

"You never listen to a word I say," she snapped at him. "Really it's too bad of you, John! Dick Hallowell ought to be on his knees to you, ready to do anything you ask. He should have resigned when his brother was arrested. It isn't very creditable to the regiment that its senior subaltern has a convict for a brother."

"Dick offered his resignation, but of course I wouldn't accept it. There would have been a riot in the mess if I had. We can't help the fool things our relatives do," the Colonel was stung to reply, and she had enough knowledge of him to be warned by his tone.

"There always has been bad blood in the Hallowells," she said. "I shouldn't be a bit surprised if Dick went like his brother."

"What rubbish you talk, my love!" said the Colonel wearily. "They are only half-brothers, anyway. Graham's mother was an out-and-out bad hat. All the crookedness that was introduced into the family came through her. Are you dining out tonight?" he asked hopefully.

"No, I'm not. And I want to tell you that Bobbie Longfellow was very rude to me the other day – most offensive."

"What did he say?"

"It wasn't what he said, it was the way he said it. His manner is insufferable. Nobody knows better than you, John, that the whole discipline of the Berwicks is slack. I'm not saying it is your fault – "

"Make up your mind whose fault it is," said the Colonel stuffily, as he got up. "I'm going to the orderly-room, my dear. I'll see you later."

When he came back for tea, as he was in duty bound to do, her ladyship had retired to her room with a headache. He sent up a sympathetic message and enjoyed his tea. Later he saw his adjutant, who pointed out three civilians who were crossing the square, one of them carrying a light ladder.

"I think the Treasury must be getting scared of the regalia," said the adjutant. "They've sent an official down from headquarters to inspect the alarm bells."

The Colonel chuckled. From time to time Whitehall had qualms of this character. Once, many years before, they had changed the strongroom door – on another occasion detectives had been sent down to question the warders about a mysterious American who had been a little too interested in the weight and value of the two big diamonds which were kept in the cage.

"I'd like to see the fellow who'd try to imitate Colonel Blood – I don't suppose there is such a man outside of a mental institution," he said.

He was in the mess, reading some Indian newspapers that had come to hand, when the phone message came for Lady Cynthia. She sent her maid back with a message that she could not be disturbed. In a few moments the girl returned.

"He says he must speak to you, madam. He's been trying ever since the tenth of June to get into touch with you."

The effect of the words on Lady Cynthia was electrical. She sat bolt upright on the bed where she had been lying, her face twitching.

"All right – I will come down. Put the phone through to the Colonel's study."

Her voice was a little husky; this the maid noticed, but saw nothing remarkable in her ladyship's change of mind. Cynthia almost ran downstairs, closed the door securely, and for five minutes was speaking in a low tone to the caller. When she came out she looked rather pale, the maid thought, but the headache was excuse enough for that.

When the Colonel returned he found his wife in the drawing-room. She was dressed for dinner and her cloak lay over the back of a chair.

"Not going out, my dear?" he asked.

"Yes; I've only just remembered an engagement I made a month ago," she said off-handedly. "It is an awful bore, but you don't mind, John?"

"Mind? Not a bit. I'll eat my dinner in solitary state, or I might dine with the mess."

One of Lady Cynthia's weaknesses was her frugality.

"Dinner has been ordered and I can't have it wasted. Ask one of the men over to dine with you," she said. "I shall be back by eleven."

The first guest that occurred to the Colonel was Dick Hallowell, but Dick was on guard. The adjutant had another engagement; he was not at the moment on polite speaking terms with the senior major. He decided to dine alone. And then, when the gong was sounding and he was strolling into the panelled room where the table had been set, came a most unexpected visitor. It was Diana Martyn, in her gayest array.

"Great heavens, Diana!" said the Colonel in amazement. "What brings you here?"

At that moment he was devoutly thankful that Lady Cynthia had gone out.

"Cynthia brought me here," was the astounding reply.

"Cynthia?" incredulously.

"She asked me to come to dinner – at least, she telephoned to my maid while I was out, and naturally I jumped at the opportunity. I'm rather fond of Cynthia, and it's one of my little troubles that she doesn't like me any more."

"But, my dear!" He was aghast at the news. "Cynthia has had to go out – an engagement she made a month ago. Too bad…"

He rang the bell for his wife's maid, but the girl did not know where her ladyship was dining.

"Set another place for Miss Martyn," said the Colonel. "Of course you'll stay, Diana!" when she demurred. "Cynthia would never forgive me if I let you go."

He was full of apologies on behalf of his wife, but on the whole he was not ill-pleased to have so charming a companion, and the dinner was a much more pleasant little function than he had ever anticipated.

Toward the end of the dinner she asked a question.

"How do you get out?" He laughed jovially. "You don't imagine you're bolted and barred in the Tower, do you, and that the sentries will first challenge and then bayonet you if you haven't the countersign?"

"It would be rather serious if I hadn't," she said. "But do you have passwords in the Tower?" she asked innocently.

He nodded.

"Yes, there's a word for all the guards in London; it is changed daily."

"Abracadabra?" she suggested with a smile.

"Nothing so complicated. The poor old guardsman would get the shock of his life if he had to remember that! No, it's usually a name of a town. Tonight it is – let me see – 'Boston,' that is it

"Boston!" She almost gasped her dismay. None of the four words that Trayne had expected.

How was she to convey the alteration? She thought it over through the rest of the dinner, and decided that it would be comparatively easy. The first time she was alone she wrote the word on a slip of paper, wrapped it round a shilling, and put it carefully into the pocket of her bag.

At ten o'clock she decided she must go. She was fortunate in her choice of time, for they were hardly out of the house before Lady Cynthia rang up to say that she would not be back until midnight.

As they walked down towards the guardroom she saw the ceremony about which she had heard often; that old-world routine which night after night, through hundreds and hundreds of years, has been observed in the Tower.

Through the grim gate of the Bloody Tower marched a small party of men, the lamplight glinting on naked bayonets, a man with a swinging lantern preceding them. A sharp voice rang out:

"Halt! Who comes there?"

The party halted, and a deep gruff voice said: "Keys."

"Whose keys?" demanded the sentry.

"King George's keys," was the reply.

Then, at the shout of the sentry, the guard turned out and lined up. She heard Dick Hallowell's deep voice cry: "Pass, King George's keys!… Guard! present arms!"

The rifles came down with a crash, and the little party marched till it came abreast, and then the old Beefeater who carried the keys removed his hat, and his voice reverberated through the deserted spaces of the Tower: "God preserve King George!"

"So that is what they call 'the keys'? she whispered to the Colonel.

"Yes; quaint, isn't it? The only night they varied the ceremony was when Queen Victoria died, and they didn't know what name the new King would take."

Her heart was beating rapidly as she passed the Jewel House. There was a sentry here, another sentry facing Traitor's Gate; farther along by the moat a third sentry, and at the outer gate yet another. Her knees were trembling beneath her as she came out into Tower Hill, and the Colonel's servant went in search of a taxi cab.

It was at that moment that a newsboy approached her. Before the Colonel could order him away –

"Yes, please," she said quickly, and slipped the coin and paper into the man's hand.

She would have forgotten to take the newspaper, but he thrust it upon her.

"I'm rather fond of – crossword puzzles," she said breathlessly, when the Colonel chided her gently upon her desire for sensational news.

She was almost fainting when the cab drove away.

17

It was past one o'clock when a motor-wherry stole out of the darkness of the Surrey shore and, describing a wide circle east of London Bridge, moved past Billingsgate, edged slowly toward the northern bank. With its engine shut off, the boat came to the stone-faced wharf of the Tower. The four men who formed her crew gripped the wharf edge, and pulled the boat along until they had passed St Thomas's Tower and were almost opposite the sentry box of the wharf sentry. Peering over, the leader of the party saw the sentry leave his shelter and, bringing his rifle to his shoulder, walk briskly towards the eastern end of his beat. The rain had ceased for the moment, but the respite would not be long. One of the men leapt up, crossed the rail, and, stooping, ran noiselessly towards the sentry box, disappearing into the gloom. Presently they heard the nailed boots of the wharf sentry returning. He stopped before his box and brought his rifle butt to the ground. What seemed to be an eternity of waiting, and then there was a muffled cry, the clatter of a falling rifle, and silence...

Another of the men lifted from the deck of the boat a light ladder, pushed it over the rails and vaulted across, followed by the other two. The last to leave was Graham Hallowell. He wore the uniform of a Guards officer, and holding his sword so that it could not rattle, he ran swiftly across the space which divided the wharf edge from the deep square well in which was placed the Traitor's Gate. He did not look to see what had become of the sentry; there was no time to think about the fate of the unfortunate man who lay unconscious upon the grass. In a second he was going down the ladder that had been dropped into the well, two rungs at a time. Somebody was working at the big spiked gates that had opened so often to receive traitor and innocent. What they were doing he could not see, but presently a voice whispered "Come" and he sidled through the open gate and found himself facing the steps immediately before the Bloody Tower.

Caution was needed here. They heard the feet of a sentry pacing up and down. In the dark he was invisible.

Again the leader slipped forward without a sound. He carried in his hand a small steel cylinder to which was affixed a flattened funnel-shaped apparatus, but Graham had neither time nor inclination to investigate this. He supposed it contained some paralysing gas, because he had seen its user cover his face with a small mica and rubber mask before he left the boat.

The clock of a City church struck the quarter-hour after one. No sound came from ahead of them as they crouched by the steps.

"Halt! Who comes there?"

Graham caught his breath. The man had been seen by the sentinel.

"Friend."

"Advance, friend, and give the countersign!"

Faintly the word came back: "Boston."

"Pass, friend – all's well."

They heard nothing more. After a while the man in the mask returned and they moved to the east, along the curtain wall.

As they passed the sentry box Graham had a glimpse of a huddled figure.

"I've put a bottle of whisky inside," said Mawsey – Graham knew the mask now – "you'll have to pretend he's drunk."

He opened the door of a small round tower, apparently an outwork that was used as a living room by some official, and into this they crowded.

"Stand by me," he whispered into Graham's ear. "When I drop your brother, take his place."

Peering round the edge of the door, he saw the twinkle of a lantern. It was Dick making his rounds to inspect the sentries.

Apparently he had been to the wharf and was now returning to the main guard. They came striding along, a drummer boy leading, carrying a lantern, two men, a non-commissioned officer, and lastly Dick. They passed the open doorway, and then: "Now!" hissed a voice in Graham's ear.

He heard no sound, but suddenly Dick seemed to crumple up. In another instant, Graham had taken the place of his stiff brother. One of the men in front of him half turned his head as though he had heard a sound.

"Look to your front!" said Graham sharply, in just the tone that he knew Dick would use. And then: "Halt!"

They had reached the sentry box opposite the Traitor's Gate. The sergeant stepped out of the ranks, and walked towards the still figure lying half in and half out of the box.

"What's the matter with that man, sergeant?" demanded Graham gruffly.

"I don't know, sir. Wake up!" He shook the inanimate figure. "It's Filpert, sir; he looks as if he's drunk."

"Bring him to the guardroom."

The two men slung their rifles and tried to drag the unconscious man to his feet. There was a distinct smell of spirits, and presently the sergeant stooped and picked up a small bottle.

"Whisky," he said, sniffing at the neck. "Put him in the guardroom."

"Shall I post one of these men here, sir?"

"No, no, it is not necessary."

They passed through the gate. Boldly he followed the group into the guardroom. Not a man there would have distinguished Graham Hallowell from his brother. Dick had a slight dark moustache. That moustache was now on Graham's upper lip, a natural growth fostered in the time of preparation.

The sergeant of the guard followed his "officer" inside.

"I'd best post another man in place of Filpert, sir," he said.

"It isn't necessary," answered Graham curtly.

The non-commissioned officer looked surprised, but made no comment. Graham was alone on the veranda, alone save for the main guard sentry. He walked up to the man, who stiffened to attention and brought his rifle to the slope as Graham approached him.

"Have a chocolate, sentry?"

The man hesitated, a little bewildered. The officers of the Berwick Guards do not as a rule wander about in the middle of the night offering their men chocolates.

"Th-thank you, sir," stammered the sentry.

Graham watched him put it in his mouth, saw him chew mechanically twice, and put his hand to his throat... Graham caught the rifle before it fell and eased him to the ground. There was no sound from the guardroom. He dragged the man to the far end of the veranda, and, leaving him in a corner, vaulted over to the roadway beneath. The sentry heard him coming, and the rattle of his rifle as it came up was Graham's warning.

"Don't challenge me," he said. "I'm Sir Richard Hallowell."

The second sentry took the chocolate with greater reluctance than the first man.

"I don't eat chocolates, sir."

"Eat it, you fool!" said his supposed officer, and the sentry obeyed.

It was the man in the mica mask who caught him as he fell.

"Go up by the guardroom door in case the sergeant comes out; and hold him in conversation," were the low instructions Graham received, and with a nod he went to his post. Well it was for the success of the enterprise that he did so, for as he stood there the door opened and the sergeant emerged.

"I'm worried about that sentry, Sir Richard," he said. "The orders about the Jewel Tower are very strict, and I shall have to put it in my report tomorrow."

"It will be all right, sergeant," said Graham coolly. "Mr Longfellow has just come in and I've asked him to tell the adjutant. I shouldn't interfere in this matter if I were you."

"Do you think there's anything wrong, sir?" asked the sergeant. "I can't understand how that man got that whisky. The men tell me that he was a teetotaller."

"There may be something radically wrong," answered Graham after a pause, "but it would be very much better if you didn't interfere."

"Very good, sir." The non-commissioned officer saluted and went back.

Looking down towards the gate, his heart going like the paddle of a river steamer, Graham Hallowell saw two dark figures emerge from the glass-covered portico of the Jewel House. There was a low whistle; it was the signal. Running noiselessly down the steps, he followed in their wake.

He had cleared the wicket of the Bloody Tower when out of the darkness somebody challenged him.

"Hallo, Dick! I want to see you."

Before he realised his danger, a lanky form stood between him and safety. It was Bobbie Longfellow.

"I couldn't see Hope. I've been looking all the evening for her – "

And here Graham, in the tense excitement of the moment, made his fatal error.

"I can't talk to you now," he said and pushed the younger man aside.

In that instant his arm was gripped. Bobbie's face peered down at him.

"By God!" gasped the young officer. "You're not Dick Hallowell!... Who are – "

Graham struck out savagely. Bobbie Longfellow relinquished his hold of the man's arm and staggered back, falling against the gate. In another second Graham was running at top speed. He leapt over the rail, sped through the open Traitor's Gate, and literally flew up the ladder. Mawsey was waiting at the top for him.

"Hurry!" he hissed.

And there was need for hurry. They heard a sharp tone of command and the sound of running feet. Even as Graham leapt from the wharf to the waiting boat –

Bang !

The first bullet whizzed by his ear.

The boat was now driving down the river at full speed. The tide was going out and was with them. Out of the shadows of the Tower Bridge a police launch shot and an authoritative voice hailed them. The boat was ahead of them, broadside on. Mawsey at the wheel slewed the sharp nose of the launch towards the police craft; there was a crash as the bow drove through the frailer boat, and almost before he was aware of what had happened, Graham saw two men struggling in the water and heard their shouts grow fainter.

Rapidly he divested himself of his uniform and threw it into the river. Beneath he was partly dressed in civilian clothing.

"Are we going all the way by water?" he asked as he struggled into a macintosh.

"No, we're going ashore this side of Deptford. They'd certainly pick us up before we reached Greenwich. All the telephones are working overtime!"

The boat was heading for the Surrey shore. Presently it slowed; a boathook gripped the edge of a wharf. Her nose was kicked off and after the last man had landed she was allowed to drift downstream. There were three cars waiting, and Mawsey, with a square black box, took the second.

Graham realised, as he was bundled inside, that it was a taxi cab.

"We can't go far in this."

"There's no need to go far," said Mawsey curtly. "Here, take this box. Have you got a gun?"

"Not with me; I have one on the ship."

Mawsey explained the immediate plan.

"I'll leave you on Blackheath. We'll find another car waiting for us there and you'll go on alone. The driver has got his instructions. You ought to be on the *Pretty Anne* before daybreak. We're sending a man by aeroplane to Ireland to foul the trail. You should have had a gun."

Graham looked at the illuminated dial of the watch on his wrist and was amazed to find that it was only half-past one. So much had happened in a quarter of an hour.

In the middle of Blackheath the taxi stopped and they alighted. A long, black car stood by the side of the road, and without a word Graham jumped inside, put his precious package by his side as an arm rest, and waited patiently for the car to start. Presently came Mawsey and passed something through the open window, which Graham took. It was a uniform cap; he felt the shiny peak of it.

"Put that on if you're stopped. You're an inspector of police going down to Gravesend to make inquiries. Good luck!"

The words were hardly out of his mouth before the car moved forward.

In his life Graham Hallowell had driven fast, but he had never had a journey like this. The machine tore along the roads. The outskirts of Bromley he recognised. They were approaching Gravesend when the car shot to the left, along the uneven surface of a lane, and, swinging round, crossed a field.

"Here you are!" The driver jerked open the door, and Graham Hallowell floundered out into a foot of mud.

It was raining heavily. He could see nothing, but somewhere at hand was the river; he could hear the wash and gurgle of water, could smell the near sea. A big hand fumbled at his shoulder.

"This way," said a harsh voice, and he recognised Eli Boss and slipped and slid down a clay embankment, at the bottom of which a little launch was bobbing and rolling.

Scrambling aboard, he sat down and the boat almost heeled over as the bulky figure of Eli Boss came after him...

He could see the *Pretty Anne* now, her starboard light throwing green spirals of reflection into the water. Nearer and nearer they approached her, and presently, passing under her stern, reached the rope ladder thrown over for their accommodation. He gripped the rope with one hand, and with great difficulty hauled himself and his precious box on to the slimy, slippery iron deck. Eli Boss joined him almost immediately. He heard the creak and strain of block and pulley as the motor launch was hauled aboard, and there commenced under his feet the thud of screws and the crazy, rackety squeak and whine of ill-used engines.

"Get below," said Eli Boss curtly. "You know your cabin? The lock's fitted – and the safe."

No light illuminated the narrow gangway, and he had to find his way to the lower deck by sense of touch. Groping along the alleyway, he reached his cabin, turned the handle. The case he put on the floor before he found his key, and feeling for the keyhole, locked himself in. Only then did he strike a light.

Both portholes had been closed with deadlights. An oil lamp was suspended in a bracket fixed to the grimy wall, and this he lit before he surveyed his new home. There had been some rough attempt to add comfort to the cheerless surroundings. An unframed oleograph had been pinned to the wall; a glaringly brand-new cloth covered the table in the centre. He saw the safe; it was in a corner of the room and clamped to the deck by steel brackets. The first duty was to put the stolen property in the safe, and he lost no time in taking this precaution. It was when the door was slammed to and the bolts had shot home that Graham Hallowell sat down and made an effort to recover his balance.

The boat was moving swiftly, he guessed, though he had no means by which he could calculate the speed, other than the rapidity and noisiness of her clanking engines. Here was the beginning of the adventure. How would it end, he wondered? What had happened to Dick?

He felt no remorse at whatever fate may have overtaken his half-brother. Dick had always hated him, he told himself – Dick, who might have done so much to make his lot a little easier. Would he be court-martialled?

There was a knock at the door, a heavy thud and then a scratching.

"Who is it?" he asked.

"Open, for God's sake!" said a hollow voice, and Graham sprang to the door, turned the key, and as he flung it wide open a ghastly, blood-covered figure collapsed against him and almost sent him flying.

It was Colley Warrington!

18

There were moments that afternoon when Hope Joyner had doubts of her wisdom. So doubtful was she, that she called up Dick Hallowell at three in the afternoon, only to learn that he was on guard.

Colley Warrington she knew as everybody knew. The story of his early exploits was public property. He had lived down his past to some extent, but there were doors still closed to him, doors that would never open. Had she consulted Dick Hallowell, Colley would never have passed the threshold of her apartment. He had come into her life largely through the instrumentality of the rajah, though she could not have guessed this, believing rather that she owed her acquaintance with Colley to the fortuitous circumstance that he was a friend of a member of her Indian committee.

It supported his suggestion that he could put her in the way of discovering something about her origin, that Colley had notoriously an encyclopaedic knowledge of the social world and the larger world which fringes that restricted area.

She might have rejected, or listened with amused contempt to, almost any other semi-stranger who dared even introduce the subject of her obscure beginning. But Colley was licensed; could and did say things which in another man would have been outrageous; and when, without preamble or warning, he had coolly asserted his right as a "friend" to share her confidences, she had been too staggered to repulse him. And before she knew what had happened, he was telling her with the greatest gravity that information had come to him about her father.

At nine o'clock that evening she found herself, largely to her own consternation, walking down Villiers Street, ready on the slightest excuse to turn back. But the excuse was not forthcoming. She saw Colley waiting for her outside the little restaurant, and suffered herself to be piloted to a table in a sparsely filled dining-room.

It was to Colley's credit, as she thought, that he ordered a simple repast, and almost before the waiter was out of earshot began his story. It was a very plausible story. It was about a woman in lowly circumstances, who had married a man of considerably higher station in life. They had quarrelled and separated, the woman to return to the secretaryship from which her marriage had rescued her. Six months after the parting, Hope had been born; and because she hated her husband, the mother had caused word to be sent to her rich husband that both she and the child had died. Believing this, Hope's father (so Colley's invention ran) had married again, to discover, to his horror, after the death of his real wife, that he had committed bigamy. He dared not confess to Hope without shattering the lives of the children that had come as the result of his second marriage. Therefore, he had arranged to keep her in luxury, without acknowledging her.

"As a matter of fact, my dear Hope," said Colley, as he sipped his red wine, "it was only with the greatest difficulty that I persuaded your father to see you."

"I am not so sure that I wish to see him," said Hope quietly.

"I thought you might say that," was his easy reply, "but in all the circumstances I think it would be foolish if you denied yourself this opportunity. I understand that your father will give you all the documents necessary to satisfy your worst enemy."

"Where is he?" she asked. "Why couldn't he come here?"

"There are many reasons," said the glib Mr Warrington, "all of which he will explain himself. Not the least of these is his extraordinary resemblance to you. It would not have been possible for you to have met without the veriest tyro who saw you together knowing that you were his daughter. What he has done is this: he has brought his motor yacht down river from Henley, and at this moment it is anchored just west of London Bridge. He is sending the motor dinghy to pick us up, and we're going aboard for half an hour."

She stared at him.

"On the river tonight? That is impossible!"

Colley shrugged his shoulders.

"I thought you might say that," he said, "and really I can't blame you. I'll be perfectly frank with you, Hope; whatever qualities I may possess, nobody has ever accused me of altruism. There's nothing in this for me, neither kudos nor money, and though I'm not particularly keen on kudos, I have a weakness for our good currency. I am utterly indifferent whether you see him or whether you don't. I thought his plan was stupid, even fantastical, but he is one of those unfortunate people who worry about what people will think of him, and I have tried to respect his scruples. If you don't wish to go any farther, we'll leave the matter where it is."

"But I must know his name," she said.

"You'll not learn it from me," said Colley quietly. "It is not in my interest to betray his confidence. If he wishes to tell you himself – well, that is his look-out."

Apparently he was indifferent, for he called to the waiter for his bill and seemed impatient to have done with the business.

"I'll go," she said. "How do we get there?"

"Do you know Upper Thames Street? It is rather a dingy waterside thoroughfare in the City of London, made up of warehouses and wharves. A few hundred yards from London Bridge is a little entry leading to some old steps – watermen's steps, as they were called – and I have arranged for the launch to be waiting for you there. But, my dear Hope, pray don't go if you feel the slightest hesitation."

He talked in this strain for another five minutes, even advised her against the experiment when he was certain that she had bitten the bait.

They went by train to the Mansion House Station and made the rest of the journey on foot, passing only one policeman, but at that moment they were so near to the centre of the traffic that the officer scarcely observed them. A few minutes later they reached a dark and narrow entry between the high walls of two warehouses, and, looking through, Hope saw the reflection of light upon water.

"Is that the boat?" she asked in a low voice. She could see the shape of it dimly.

"I expect so," said Colley. "I'll go and inquire. The motor yacht is farther out..."

"Don't leave me," she said nervously, and followed him down the entry...

"The steps are rather slippery," he said as he put out his hand to steady her.

It was a tiny launch; there was scarcely room for the two of them to sit in the stern; and as it went "chug-chugging" into the open water she searched the river for anything that had the appearance of a motor yacht that would pass muster at Henley. And of such craft there was no sign.

"It's a little farther down," said Colley readily.

Without warning he turned on her. One hand went about her throat, the other covered her mouth, and one of the two men who formed the crew of the launch gripped at her ankles and pulled. She tried to struggle, but the weight of Colley Warrington was lying across her, and she felt herself slipping into the darkness of death...

"The only danger is a police launch," said the husky voice of Joab Boss – Eli's son. "There's generally one nosing about the wharves, but they keep to the Surrey side."

The rain was pelting down. Colley, in his thin macintosh, shivered as he sat, moistening the chloroform cone that he held over the girl's white face.

"It's a funny thing," said Joab, "but the old man thought she was going to give more trouble than – "

"Than what?" asked Colley.

"Nothing," growled the man. "Don't be too inquisitive, mister. He didn't think you'd get her so easily. She must be a fool; but all women are fools. How far is she going?"

"To India."

He heard Joab whistle.

"India, eh? The old man didn't tell me that."

A long silence, during which apparently he ruminated upon a new and dangerous situation.

"It's a pity," he said. "The old man's funny...but I don't suppose, after his last trouble, he'll take any risks."

Colley Warrington did not ask him what was the last trouble in which Eli Boss was involved. If he had, the final flickering spark of mercy in his soul might have induced him to lift the girl from the bottom of the boat and drop her into the river.

"He's funny, the old man...where wimmin are concerned. Somebody will get into trouble over this, won't they?" he asked, after another long silence. "Suppose you rounded on us?"

"I betray you?" said Colley dryly. "I'm hardly likely to."

Joab said no more till they were off Greenwich, and then, coming back to the aft part of the launch, he squatted down at the feet of the unconscious girl.

"What's she like for looks?" he asked. "I couldn't see her in the dark."

"She's pretty enough," said the other, and he heard the sailor growl something under his breath.

"What did you say?"

"I don't know... I wish she wasn't coming. The old man's a fool where wimmin are concerned."

"I'm going too," said Colley.

"Are you?" was the reply, rather than a question.

The passenger tried to get from him some particulars about the boat; what arrangements had been made for his accommodation.

"Better ask the old man," was the cautious answer. "He saw that coon yesterday, or two days ago."

"He saw the Prince?" asked Colley in surprise.

"No, not the Prince – another coon."

The secretary probably, thought Colley.

"He's had his orders, whatever they are... I never ask questions and I don't hear no lies. The only thing I can tell you about it is that I wish she wasn't coming. He's very peculiar to wimmin – if they're good-lookers," he added after a pause.

For the first time that evening Warrington began to feel uneasy. He was not concerned very much over the safety or danger of the girl whose head lay on his knee. That did not trouble him. What sort of a life would he live on this rotten old tub, with a brute of a skipper who was "very peculiar to wimmin"? He wished he had never touched the business. Perhaps at the last he could get out of going to India on the ship. There might be orders for him on board. He sincerely hoped there would be.

It was nearly one o'clock when, peering ahead, Joab passed the word back that the *Pretty Anne* was in sight. She carried one dim light, and so far as they could see, approaching her from the stern, there was no kind of illuminant at all to help them up her rusty side. A gruff voice from the deck hailed them.

"That you, Joab?"

"Yes, old man."

"Got her?"

"Yeh."

"Make fast to the launch. Do you come up, Joab. Sammy!"

"Yes, sah?"

The second member of the crew was evidently a negro from his voice.

"Pass this line round the young woman." Something fell with a smack on the launch, and Colley lifted the girl whilst the negro adjusted the noose around her waist.

"Make fast, sah."

"She's asleep, ain't she? Doped?"

"Yes," said Colley, and watched the slim figure hauled out of sight to the deck above.

"Come right up, Sammy."

The negro scrambled nimbly up the side of the ship, after fastening the bow of the boat to the ladder.

"Now come up – you!"

Colley grasped the rope and began a laborious ascent. One arm was flung across the bulwarks, a foot was being raised to follow, when Eli Boss spoke.

"Don't come inboard yet."

There was no light to see his face, but Colley Warrington caught the aroma of a spirit-laden breath.

"You stay just where you are a minute."

"Why?" asked Colley, both hands gripping the rail.

"Because I'm telling you," growled Eli Boss. "There's too many people aboard as it is."

Colley Warrington felt rather than saw the swing of the marlinspike; and ducked, but not soon enough. Something struck his head, and the shattering pain of the blow made him release his hold and he dropped like a stone into the river. The cold of the water revived him for a second. He struck out wildly and presently his fingers touched a slimy chain, to which he held with the tenacity of death. He felt the warm blood flowing down his face, but, setting his teeth, he drew himself up hand over hand by the mooring chain. The strain was intolerable; at every move he had an aching desire to release his hold and find rest and freedom from pain in the river.

Rikisivi had done this; his old trick of destroying evidence… Eli Boss would never have dared. He must live.

He clawed upwards, gripped broken wire and felt his hands lacerated; reached higher and caught a rail, and, exerting the last atom of his reserve of strength, wriggled and squirmed his way on to the poop deck before he fainted.

This was the story he told.

Graham Hallowell listened, horrified.

"Hope Joyner here?" he said. "You swine!"

"Hide me! You've got to hide me!" Colley's teeth were chattering with fear and cold. The white, blood-streaked face was ghastly to see. "He'll kill me…and he'll kill you too, Hallowell."

A footstep sounded in the alleyway, and Graham thought quickly. Beneath the bed was a long locker that ran its length. Storage space he saw as he looked down. It was empty. Lying on the deck, the wretched Colley rolled himself out of sight, and the flap had hardly been fastened when the door opened and Eli Boss came in.

"Got your 'coke' in, eh?" he asked, glancing at the safe, and reminded Graham that the ostensible reason for the trip was to convey cocaine to India. "I thought you was going to have a travelling pal, a fellow named Colley something – he had to turn back. Got everything you want?"

Graham's portmanteau was lying on the bed.

"You'll find stowage for that under the bunk. That all you've got?"

"That is all I want," said Graham.

As the captain turned to go, an idea occurred to the passenger.

"I'd like a gun," he said.

The old man turned his bloated face and his eyes were like slits.

"Want a gun, do you? What do you want a gun for?"

"I might find it useful," said Graham coolly.

"Ain't you got one?" Without further ado, his big hand pawed Graham Hallowell's hip in search of a weapon. "Huh! Thought you'd have one," he said, and there was just a gleam of satisfaction in the snake-like eyes. "We don't want any guns on this packet, mister. Nobody's coming aboard, and nobody's going to hurt you. We're out of the river." The information was unnecessary, for the *Pretty Anne* was rolling and wallowing in the trough of the North Sea.

He slammed the door behind him and went out. The clatter of his heavy feet came fainter and fainter. Graham went quickly to the bed and examined the portmanteau. Some sort of attempt had been made to open it; he saw that by the scratches on the hasp, but the attempts had ended in failure, for the locks were unpickable and the portmanteau had been specially chosen for this reason. He fastened the door of the cabin before he threw open the leather lid and retrieved the long Browning and packet of ammunition that he had packed. With the magazine charged and in his pocket, he felt a little easier in his mind, and then remembered Colley Warrington suffocating beneath the box and went to his aid.

The man was on the point of fainting when he dragged him out on to the deck.

"Did you hear him?"

Colley shook his head, incapable of speech.

"He said you went back. Now tell me, where is Hope Joyner?"

"I don't know – somewhere on the ship. They took her aboard before they knocked me out."

"How did you get her here? Well, I won't ask that now. But you'll tell me, Colley, and, by God! if anything happens to that girl, there's only one place of refuge for you, and that's with Eli Boss!"

He made a quick search of the cabin, tried the handle of the door in one of the bulkheads, and found that it led to a smaller cabin. Eli had promised him a bathroom and had kept his word; there was a ragged hose dangling from what he supposed was a waterpipe, and an old locker; otherwise the cabin was empty. It had the advantage of being cut off from the alleyway, for there was no connecting door except that which opened into Graham Hallowell's "suite."

"You get in there. Here's a towel. You can have a couple of blankets and one of these pillows. I think you'll be safe for the night if I lock you in."

"Give me some water!" gasped the wretch, and Graham handed him a water bottle from the rack.

With the gun in his pocket, Graham stepped out into the alleyway, locked the door behind him and made his unsteady way to the open air. The *Pretty Anne* was leaping and tossing in a half-gale of wind which had swept down from the north east. On the starboard quarter he could see a rim of glittering lights, and guessed it to be a popular seaside resort. He was standing by the side, gripping a stanchion to prevent his being thrown to the deck with every lurch that the old tub gave, when Eli Boss clattered down from the upper deck into the well, where Graham was.

"You get to bed," he said roughly. "I don't want nobody about tonight."

With his arm about the stanchion, Hallowell turned.

"I'll get to bed when I damn well please," he said without heat. "Is that understood, Boss? And listen!" Before the big man could recover from his astonishment: "I'm going out as a passenger. You're well paid for what you're doing, and part of your payment is for civility. I'm out of Dartmoor – perhaps you don't know that – and in Dartmoor there are lions that make you look like a rabbit! Get that thought into your system, my man."

His hand gripped the butt of his Browning, but this, Eli Boss did not know. The bullying shipmaster was cowed, not by any evidence of material superiority, but by the voice of a man who had once been a gentleman.

"Don't let's have any arguments, mister," he said almost humbly. "If you want a bit of fresh air, you shall have it! Don't interfere with me and I won't interfere with you."

"I'll interfere just when I want," said Graham. "Your job is to navigate this ship to a port – that's your job. And whilst you're doing that you won't be interfered with. There's a girl on this ship, Captain, and I have orders to look after her. That is my business, and if you interfere with me you'll be sorry."

Eli Boss opened his mouth to say something, changed his mind and went blundering up the ladder to his own place, which was the bridge of the *Pretty Anne*.

19

It was Bobbie who found Dick Hallowell, lying huddled against the inner wall of a small bastion. He was unconscious, and Bobbie lifting him to his shoulder, carried him back to the guardroom and laid him down on one of the plank beds, whilst men of the guard went off in search of the doctor and the Colonel.

Colonel Ruislip had not retired; he was sitting in the drawing room, waiting for the return of his wife, when the guardsman came to report, and he was by Dick's side before the doctor arrived. And now he heard from the sergeant of the guard the strange story of the three doped sentries. It was some minutes after this that the sergeant of the "spur" guard discovered the fourth sentry on the wharf.

Curiously enough, the robbery was not immediately discovered; for the thief had coolly locked the outer door before he had fled with his booty.

"But they were after the regalia, that's certain. My God, what a dreadful thing to have happened!"

They had taken off Dick's coat and tunic, and he lay very white and still whilst the four men of the guard were stretched on the floor, in no better case. The doctor, a war veteran, came in at that moment, a trench coat over his pyjamas, and he made a brief examination.

"Gas of some kind," he said, as he sniffed the tunic and went on to inspect the unfortunate guardsmen, one of whom was recovering under the application of a wet sponge to his face.

From him they learnt the story of the officer and the chocolates.

"It wasn't Dick, of course," said Bobbie quickly. "It was the fellow I mistook for him. In some way he managed to take Dick's place – Heaven knows how."

He questioned the sergeant of the guard and heard from the sentry the story of the slight scuffling noise he had heard.

"…then the officer told me to look to my front," said the man.

"That is when it occurred!" Bobbie nodded.

The Colonel beckoned the drummer of the guard to him.

"Sound the Assembly," he said, and to Bobbie: "Take control of the guard until you're relieved. Double all sentries; no person is to enter or leave the Tower except by my orders."

He went down the steps, a greatly troubled man, and was making his way to his quarters, wondering as to which member of the Government he should telephone, when he heard his name called, and turning, saw a woman walking quickly towards him. It was his wife.

"What is wrong, John?" she asked anxiously.

"Come on, I'll tell you."

As they walked side by side towards the house, he explained what had happened.

"The regalia?" she gasped. "Surely not…that is impossible!"

"I hope so," he said grimly. "We shall know in a few minutes when the Constable arrives."

As he spoke, the blare of the bugle sounding the Assembly rang out in the dark, and before he reached his house he saw lights appearing in the barrack-room and the officers' quarters.

"Where have you been, my dear? Why are you so late?"

It was not customary of him to ask such a question in so sharp a tone; less than usual for Lady Cynthia to reply so meekly.

"I've been to dine with somebody I haven't seen for over twenty years," she said. "It was entirely a private matter, and I would rather you didn't ask me any more about it."

The Colonel was too astonished to reply. As he was telephoning, he looked across to his wife, and was startled at the change which had come to her face. She looked old and drawn; there were heavy circles about her eyes, and that manner of insolent assurance which he knew so well seemed to have gone with the colour from her face.

He made his report, went up to his room and changed into his uniform. Lady Cynthia, standing like a frozen statue in the hall, watched him coming down the stairs buckling his sword-belt. The parade was alive now with men; as the Colonel came out of his quarters he heard the thud of rifle butts on the gravel, the sharp words of company commanders. He was striding across the square when the adjutant overtook him.

"Oh, is that you, Ferraby?" he said awkwardly. "I want twenty men and two officers to reinforce the Guard; the remainder to stand fast."

He reached the guardroom at the same time as the deputy Constable and senior warder, and together they opened the door of the Wakefield Tower and went inside. The deputy went first up the stairs, and hearing his exclamation, the Colonel's heart sank.

"The strongdoors are open!"

They followed the deputy into the jewel chamber. One glance at the centre cage was sufficient. The shutters were up, but all the jewels save the second crown were intact. There was no sign of breakage; apparently the thieves knew the secret by which the shutters were raised and dropped.

Scotland Yard had been the first notified of the event, and as he left the Wakefield Tower the Colonel was called to pass in the first carload of detectives that had arrived from the Embankment. He gave the necessary permission and returned to the guardroom. Dick Hallowell was in the officers' room, sitting in a chair. He still looked haggard and shaken, but apparently was suffering no drastic after-effects from the attack.

"I don't know what happened," he said. "I remember smelling a whiff of musty air that seemed to be blown across my face, and then I must have fainted. It was a perfectly ridiculous thing to have done."

He looked at the Colonel's grave face.

"What happened, sir?" he asked.

"Part of the regalia has been stolen," said the Colonel.

For a second, Dick Hallowell thought he was under the spell of a bad dream, and he passed his hand across his eyes as though to make sure that he was awake.

"The second crown went," said the Colonel. "Somebody put you out, and one of the scoundrels, apparently wearing the uniform of a Guards officer, took your place."

"The crown!" Dick rose to his feet, steadying himself by the edge of the table. "Who – who took my place?"

The question was flung at Bobbie.

"I don't know." Bobbie Longfellow did not meet the eyes of his friend. "I'm not sure that I should recognise him again; it was quite dark – "

"Did you hear his voice?" asked Dick quietly.

"Yes, I heard his voice."

A deadly silence followed, which Dick broke.

"It was Graham, of course?"

Bobbie did not answer.

"Graham! Our voices are almost alike, but you would know the difference. Didn't the alarm bell ring in the guardroom?"

In the excitement of the moment even the Colonel had forgotten the alarm bells. The sergeant of the guard was sent for and was very emphatic.

"No, sir, no alarm rang." The senior warder had the same story to tell. It was Bobbie Longfellow, however, who found a simple solution to the mystery. With the aid of a ladder he examined the bell in the guardroom, and at the first glance he saw the cause. The hammer was a circle of metal at the end of a steel rod, rather like an inverted pendulum. The rod had been cut off close and the pivot on which it worked was found to be held tight by little wooden wedges. Other alarm bells proved to have been similarly treated. It was as clear as daylight what had happened. The official visit of inspection, though the "inspector" had had the support of all the necessary documents, was part of the scheme. The "inspector" had gone from bell to bell and had put every one out of action.

Dick Hallowell was not surprised, when he was relieved by another officer, to learn, after a quiet talk with the adjutant, that he was under open arrest. That was an inevitable formality. He had been in command of the guard when the great jewel had been stolen, and he must answer for his responsibility. He went to his room sick at heart and weary of body, and shortly after Bobbie Longfellow joined him.

"I don't think there is much doubt as to whether I shall leave the Army or not," said Dick grimly. "After this happening, I shall be lucky if they let me resign my commission!" Then, with a weary gesture, he dismissed the ugly prospect. "Did you see Hope?"

Bobbie shook his head.

"She was out; had gone to keep some engagement and hadn't turned up when I left."

"What time did you leave?"

Bobbie thought.

"My last call was at one o'clock. The night porter told me that she hadn't returned, and I was so worried that I went up to make sure."

"And she hadn't?" asked Dick, in alarm.

"No," said Bobbie. "I was rather upset about it; in fact, I was talking to you, as I thought, on the subject, when I spotted – " He hesitated.

"Graham," said Dick evenly.

"I suppose it was Graham." Bobbie was cautious. "Anyway, I couldn't swear to him."

Dick Hallowell looked at his watch; it was a few minutes after two, and, taking up the telephone, he called a number.

"Very sorry, sir," said the operator's voice. "We have instructions not to pass out any calls from the Tower tonight."

The two men looked at one another, For a moment Dick Hallowell forgot about his own trouble and the shadow of tragedy which overcast his life, in his anxiety and concern for the girl.

"There is nothing very remarkable about her being late," he said uneasily. "She is probably dancing somewhere – "

"She wasn't dressed for dancing," blurted Bobbie, and added hastily: "She may be staying with somebody."

Dick shook his head.

"Do you think that you can get out of the Tower, Bobbie?" he asked quickly. "I am under open arrest and it is impossible for me."

Bobbie looked doubtful at this.

"Wait till I've changed," he said, and disappeared into his room. When he came back, ten minutes later, he was in uniform.

"I'm going to report to the Colonel, and if I find any excuse for leaving this grisly prison, I'll jump at it!"

The excuse was made for him, for no sooner had he joined the little circle of interested officials that had gathered in the officers' guardroom when Colonel Ruislip drew him aside.

"The Minister of War is out of town," he said in a low voice, "but the Under Secretary has been on the phone and has asked me to send an officer with a statement of all the facts, to give him material for reply in the House of Commons tomorrow. Go along and see him, Longfellow; here are the names of the sentries who were drugged, approximately the hour, and their statements. You will be able to explain to him the routine of Tower duties, the guard system we have; in fact, you can give him most of the information he will need."

"Where is he living, sir?"

And then the miracle happened.

"He has a flat in Devonshire House – which is fortunate."

Bobbie thought it was very fortunate indeed. He had no chance of going back to see Dick, but, scribbling a note, sent it across to him by an orderly.

One of the police cars was placed at his disposal, and he sped across Eastcheap, where the first of the Billingsgate vans were beginning to gather, and in something under a quarter of an hour he was in the vestibule of the apartments. His first question had nothing to do with the Under Secretary of State for War.

The porter shook his head.

"No, sir, the young lady hasn't come in yet. Her maid talks about reporting the matter to the police."

Bobbie's heart sank; for somehow, at the back of his mind, he had a feeling that all was not well with Hope Joyner. His perturbation was so great that he turned to walk out into Piccadilly, and only remembered that he was on an official visit when the porter asked him if he had come from the Tower. The elevator carried him up to the suite of the politician, and Bobbie spent an exasperating hour explaining to a rather dull, middle-aged man events which, from Bobbie's point of view, needed no explanation at all.

"This is a very serious business," said the Under Secretary, for the dozenth time. "I really don't know how the Cabinet will look at this. No word must get to the newspapers – you understand?"

"I understand, sir," said Bobbie icily (he had all the soldier's antipathy to politicians). "But will a few hundred guardsmen, a hundred or so Tower workers, and a handful of detectives also understand?"

The Under Secretary was impervious to sarcasm; possibly he did not, in his most extravagant mood, imagine that a subaltern would be guilty of such.

"An announcement will be issued to the Press in due course," he said, "but no interviews must be granted, and the soldiers must be warned on this point."

It was daylight before Bobbie was dismissed. For an hour he had been chafing, his mind upon Hope Joyner, and no sooner had he left the Under Secretary's flat than he hurried to the girl's apartments for the latest news. He found the heavy-eyed maid in tears. Hope had not returned, and there was no message from her. Bobbie Longfellow returned to the Tower with a heavy heart, and, having reported to his chief, he made a beeline for Dick Hallowell's quarters.

He found Dick lying asleep on his bed; but at the turning of the handle he opened his eyes and was on his feet in an instant.

"Well?" he asked, and very briefly Bobbie told him all he knew about the girl's disappearance. Dick Hallowell listened with a grave face.

"I don't know what to make of it," he said, when the young officer had finished. "There is just a chance that she has gone out of town, though she would have certainly told her maid."

He walked up and down the long room, his chin on his breast, and the weary Bobbie, sprawling in a deep armchair, alternately nodded and yawned. Suddenly his friend stopped.

"Bobbie," he said, "I wonder if the embargo has been lifted from the telephone?"

"Yes," said Bobbie, now wide awake. "I meant to tell you that. Officers may phone. In fact, so far as I know, anybody may phone."

He did not know that the moment the detectives had arrived at the Tower, all restrictions as to phoning had been removed. Three experts had been sent to the exchange to listen in to every conversation.

"I'm going to call up Diana," said Dick, turning the leaves of the directory.

"Diana?" said Bobbie, open-eyed with wonder. "Do you think she would know?"

"She may know – something."

"But suppose she talks about Graham – ?"

Dick cut short his objection.

"I've already told the police that in my opinion the man who impersonated me was my brother," he said quietly. "I did not tell them about Diana, because I do not exactly know their relationship. I have a sort of an idea, but I may be wrong, that Graham married her after the – trouble. That they were lovers even when she was engaged to me, I learnt to my sorrow."

He called Diana's number, and it was significant that her voice answered him almost at once.

"Dick Hallowell speaking... Diana, do you know what has happened to Hope Joyner?"

Obviously the question took her aback, because she did not answer for a moment, and when she did the surprise in her voice was genuine.

"Hope Joyner? I don't know – why? What has happened to her?"

"She left her apartments last night and has not been seen since," said Dick. "Diana, are you sure?"

"How absurd! Of course I'm sure. I never see her. Why should you ask me?" A pause. "Is anything very wrong…at the Tower?"

She was not referring now to Hope; he was certain of that.

"Where is Graham?" he asked, and her answer came too readily.

"I haven't seen him since the day before yesterday – why?" And then again: "What has happened? Why are you up so very early?"

"I can't tell you that. Diana, will you do something for me? Will you go along to Devonshire House and see if it's humanly possible to trace her?"

She considered this request before she answered.

"Yes, Dick, I'll do that. Why did you want to know about Graham? Is he in – in any kind of trouble?"

"I'm not sure," he replied. "Ring me up and tell me if you can find out anything about Hope."

The newspapers had already come into the Tower, but not even the late morning editions had any word about the robbery. At nine o'clock that morning a council was held in the Colonel's room, at which Dick attended. One of the War Office military chiefs had arrived from the country and had already gone through and sifted the written evidence.

"There is no reason why Sir Richard should remain even under open arrest," he said. "If there is one thing clearer than another, it is that he is as much a victim as any of the four sentries."

Dick learnt that the boat which had brought the robbers to the Tower had been found drifting in the Thames. The wharf at which they had landed had been identified by a policeman who in the early hours of the morning saw two cars and a taxicab drive away, and had reported the unusual circumstances. Another, and, as the police regarded it, an important clue, was discovered. The night before, a private aeroplane had been chartered from one of the flying grounds to be in readiness to leave at daybreak for a non-stop run to Ireland. In the first light of the dawn a car had arrived from which a man carrying a big bag descended. He gave his name as "Thompson," and the machine had left immediately and had landed at the Curragh, where another car was waiting to carry the passenger to an unknown destination. A more vital fact was that the mysterious passenger had left behind him a pocketbook containing a small amount of money and a blueprint plan of the Tower of London, bearing certain markings which were unintelligible to the Irish police.

"It almost looks," said Inspector Wills, who was in the conference, "as though this is our bird. The car that went to Croydon corresponds to one of the three which left the wharf. We've asked the Irish police to send the plan to us by aeroplane and it should be in our hands very soon. It may of course be a blind to throw us off the real trail. On the other hand, Ireland is one of the few countries one would expect the thieves to make for in its present turbulent state."

It so happened that Ireland at that moment was particularly tranquil, but to the average Englishman Ireland is a land of perennial unrest.

What puzzled the police was the fact that the thieves had not disturbed the remainder of the regalia. There were articles there of immense value and easy to carry, but they had contented themselves with the crown, which, whilst it was tremendously valuable, had also the most historic interest.

Another find was the discovery of a small steel cylinder containing a gas of an unknown character, and such experiments as they had been able to conduct pointed unmistakably to this being the method employed by the raiders to overcome Dick and his unfortunate sentries.

It was eleven o'clock, and Dick was trying to eat a belated breakfast, when his telephone bell rang. It was Diana, and her voice was shrill and agitated.

"Is that you, Dick?... Can you tell me anything...about Graham?"

"Nothing," he said.

Before his lips could frame the question, she went on: "I can learn nothing about Hope. She went out last night and hasn't come back... and, Dick, Colley Warrington has gone."

The full significance of this did not appear to him immediately.

"Colley Warrington?"

"Yes...yes, yes," she said impatiently. "Don't you understand? He has been very interested in Hope lately. I can't tell you more, Dick. I'm worried ill!"

"But what has Colley Warrington to do with it?" he asked.

"Dick, he wanted her for somebody" – her voice was almost a wail. "Don't you understand? Somebody was very keen on Hope."

"Kishlastan?" he asked quickly, and went white.

"I can't tell you who – I'm making such a mess of it. I'm just mad with worry."

And then abruptly she rang off. He tried to get her again, but there was no answer, and he guessed she had put down her receiver, an old and irritating trick of hers.

Kishlastan! The picture he conjured in his mind set his brain reeling. He called the exchange and asked to be put through to the hotel, though he had an idea that the Prince had already left London. This was confirmed by the reception clerk.

His Excellency, he said, had left a week before, on the *Polta*.

20

When Colonel Ruislip brought the news to his wife that Sir Richard Hallowell had been released from open arrest, she was something like her old self again.

"The fools!" she stormed. "Of course he was in it – up to his neck in it! Why was Diana here last night? His old flame? I never invited her. She must have known – "

She stopped suddenly.

"She must have known you were going out. How did she know that? Whom did you dine with?"

"Did you tell her anything about the regalia or the Tower?" She evaded the question. "Think, John."

"Tell Diana?" He frowned. "No, I don't think...by Jove, yes, I did! I gave her the countersign!"

"Ah!" Lady Cynthia leaned back, a smile of triumph on her face. "Don't you see now that she was in the plot? Why did she choose the night that Dick Hallowell was on guard?"

"Whom did you dine with last night?" he asked quietly, and this time there was no getting round the question.

She thought for a long time before she answered.

"I'll tell you the truth, John," she said. "I dined with nobody! Someone – who knew my father and my late husband – asked me to meet them, and told me the matter was urgent. Like a fool, I went, expecting to be away at the most two hours. The person I had to see was not at the – at the restaurant, but had left a message asking me to go on with the dinner and he would come in later. I waited till half past nine, and then another message came, saying that he had been taken ill and asking me if I would go and see him. I went to – to his house, and was shown into the drawing-room and asked to wait. Nobody came to me, and after a little time I decided to go back to the Tower. I then found that the door was locked. As I tried the handle, a piece of paper was put under the door with a few words, telling me not to give trouble or – "

She did not reveal the threat.

"He knew something about you, something about the past?" said the Colonel in a low voice.

She nodded.

"And he threatened to make it known if– "

"Yes, that is it. Do you want me to tell you what it was?"

He shook his head.

"I think I know, Cynthia," he said. "I'm not exactly a fool, and when we were married I had heard things, but thought it would be best for both of us if no reference was made to the past. I wish you had taken me into your confidence."

She sighed deeply.

"I wish I could have guessed you knew," she said.

"You did not see him?"

She shook her head.

"At one o'clock the door was unlocked and I left the flat without seeing a soul."

The Colonel filled his pipe and lit it with a hand that shook a little, and did not speak until he had sent a puff of smoke to the ceiling.

"You wouldn't like to tell me his name?"

She made a gesture of despair.

"You would be no wiser if I told you," she said. "He was a man I knew when I was a young girl – a wild, mysterious, lawless sort of man. My father said that he was a crook, and I think he was. He always had a great deal of money, lived like a gentleman, but there were queer stories about him, even when he was at Oxford."

The Colonel dropped his hand on her shoulder.

"Poor old girl!" he said huskily, and it needed but that to dissolve this frigid woman, and in another instant she was sobbing on his breast.

If there was one actor in the overnight drama who was apparently unperturbed by the events, known and unknown, guessed and undreamed of, it was Tiger Trayne. At eleven o'clock he sat at his breakfast, a newspaper propped against a cruet before him, his reading glasses fixed on his nose. His coffee was a little unpalatable, he complained to the man who waited on him. He had also some criticism to make about a spot of mud that had not been brushed from his trousers. He was, in fact, concerned chiefly with the minor irritations of life. The man brought him a box of cigars and he selected one with considerable care. Leaning back in his chair, he smoked leisurely, his eyes going slowly down the Stock Exchange columns. Seeing him, one might imagine that he had not a single big care in the world except for his creature comforts. There was the faint tinkle of a bell and the man went out of the room, came back, closing the door behind him.

"Will you see Mrs Ollorby, sir?"

Tiger Trayne folded his paper, put it down, took off his glasses and polished them with a silk handkerchief, all very slowly and deliberately.

"Yes, I will see Mrs Ollorby," he said. "Ask her to come in here."

He was standing with his back to the marble fireplace, a cigar between his teeth, a quizzical smile in his eyes, when the stout lady was ushered into the room and left alone with him. Mrs Ollorby appeared to have slept that night in her clothes; her face was a little grimy, but redder than ever; her big nose and protruding chins a little more conspicuous in consequence. He had seen Mrs Ollorby many times, but never quite as untidy as she was at that moment – and he suspected that certain events at the Tower of London might be responsible for her array.

"Good morning, Mrs Ollorby; this is an unexpected pleasure – and how is Hector?" he asked blandly.

"I have just sent him home; the poor boy's nearly dead. What with rowing about the river in the middle of the night – and I'm no light weight to pull, Mr Trayne – and what with the rain and the excitement and what-not, I wonder I'm not dead too."

"Sit down, won't you?"

He was not smiling now. The presence of Mrs Ollorby on the river at midnight might very well spell ruin to all his plans. He knew the woman rather well, and had had experience of her roundabout preambles and her passion for roving around a subject before she came to the point.

"It is hardly the weather, is it, for midnight boating?" he asked.

"It isn't, and that's a fact," said Mrs Ollorby, as she sat down, and rummaged in her big bag before she found a somewhat discoloured handkerchief to wipe her face. "Hector said: 'Ma, if this is detectiving I'm going to give it up.' You've no idea how strong the current is, Mr Trayne, and as we went under London Bridge I thought that the boat would upset and we'd all be drowned. They tell me fat people float naturally, but I wouldn't like to try it."

"What were you doing on the river – in the night?"

"That's what Hector said," nodded Mrs Ollorby. "He said: 'What's the use, ma? They've got a motorboat and all we've got is a pair of oars' – I wish we hadn't found that rowboat, but it was tied up to the steps and I simply couldn't resist the temptation of going out to see where they went. It wasn't so hard to trail them, because Thames Street is a pretty dark street, and I was quite near to them when he talked about the motor yacht."

Trayne frowned.

"Motor yacht?

Mrs Ollorby nodded solemnly.

"According to what he said, it was farther out – in midstream, so we oughtn't to have had far to pull. And then I thought it might be below the bridge, as they went that way. We didn't get ashore till nearly one o'clock, and then we were landed on a wharf where there were dogs, and the gate was locked and we couldn't get out till the workmen came this morning. But as I said to Hector, 'I'm not going to trust my life in that boat any more.' "

Tiger Trayne laughed softly.

"It looks to me, Mrs Ollorby, as though you had been following a snark and had found a boojum – in fact, that you were on a false scent. But why have you come to me?"

True to her principles, Mrs Ollorby did not return a direct answer.

"I didn't get home to my place till seven, and then I dozed off for a few hours. If I hadn't had those forty or fifty winks I'd have been a wreck. I suppose you think I look a bit of a wreck now?"

"You look your charming self," said Trayne ironically, and she bent her head to acknowledge the compliment.

"When I woke up, I thought it over and I said to myself – Hector being fast asleep, poor boy – The best thing I can do is to go along and see Mr Trayne and put the matter to him, because – you know how inquisitive I am," she said apologetically, "always putting my nose into other people's business – because I happen to be aware of certain things about Mr Trayne, and I'm quite sure that he doesn't like Colley Warrington."

"Colley Warrington?" Trayne spun round at the word. "What's Colley Warrington got to do with it?"

"He was with her."

" 'Her'? Who?" The words came like two clangs of a hammer upon a deep bell.

"With Miss Joyner."

She thought his eyes were shut, but he was looking at her with fierce intensity.

"Now tell me the story from the beginning. You followed Colley Warrington and Miss Joyner – to where?"

"To one of those little openings in Upper Thames Street. He had a motor boat there, and he said he was taking her out to see somebody who was in a yacht."

"What time was this?"

"As near eleven as makes no difference," she answered.

"They went downstream, you say? Did – the lady go willingly?"

"She got into the boat willingly, though I have an idea she'd rather not have gone," said Mrs Ollorby.

He had thrown his cigar into the fire. His big face was like something carved in grey stone.

"She went downstream, eh, in a motor launch? You didn't happen to hear any of the men in the launch talking?"

"Yes, I did. And do you know, Mr Trayne, it sounded very much like the voice of that big son of Eli Boss."

He took out his watch and looked at the face. She thought the action was mechanical, but there was nothing mechanical in anything Tiger Trayne did.

"It couldn't have been an elopement," Mrs Ollorby rattled on, "because this young lady's in love with Dick Hallowell."

"With Dick Hallowell?"

Horror and incredulity were in his tone.

"Do you mean Sir Richard Hallowell, the guardsman?"

She nodded.

"They were going to be married, a little bird told me. He was leaving the regiment because there was some trouble about her having no relations – though I think I could have told them something." She dropped her head on one side coyly, like an obese lovebird.

He pressed a bell in the wall.

"Thank you, Mrs Ollorby. You're a queer devil, and I dare say you're hoping to put me just where the rats won't bite, eh? Well, I'm going to put myself there: that'll interest you. Now tell me, truthfully, why did you come? Why have you told me this?"

Mrs Ollorby licked her lips.

"I'm a mother," she said. "That's enough."

He held out his hand and gripped hers, and, strong woman as she was, she winced under the pressure.

His man had come into the room.

"My car," he said, and without a word to Mrs Ollorby, he stalked out and into his bedroom.

Unlocking a drawer, he took out an automatic, examined the magazine and slipped it into his hip pocket, sought and found three reserve magazines and disposed them carefully in his waistcoat. Coming out of the hall, he lifted his overcoat and hat in passing, and saw Mrs Ollorby standing in the doorway.

"I shall remember you," he said, and was gone before she could reply.

The car went all too slowly through the crowded City streets, and he sprang out before it had come to a standstill near the closed gate of the Tower.

"I'm very sorry, sir, you can't go in," said the policeman at the door. "The Tower's closed to visitors today."

"I've an important message for Sir Richard Hallowell," said Trayne. "I must see him at once."

The policeman called another, who escorted him to the first guarded gate.

"You can take him in," said the sergeant, "but he must go straight to Sir Richard's quarters and speak to nobody."

The reason for these precautions was no mystery to the Tiger. He scarcely gave a glance at the Jewel House as he mounted the steps of the big parade ground.

"Trayne? Trayne? I know the name," said Dick, when the visitor was announced to him. "Bring him in. The policeman had better wait outside."

Tiger Trayne swung into the room, the door slammed behind him, and for a moment they looked at one another, face to face, master crook and the lover of Hope Joyner.

"Well," said Dick. "What can I do for you, Mr Trayne?"

As he asked, he remembered the man and his peculiar reputation.

"There were two robberies last night. I've come to speak to you about the most important," said the Tiger tersely. "Hope Joyner has been carried off: I suppose you know that?"

"I don't know it; I didn't want to think it," said the white-faced Dick. "Is it true?"

The man nodded curtly.

"She was fond of you?"

What right he had to ask, Dick Hallowell did not question.

"I love her," he said simply. "Why do you ask?"

The Tiger stared out through the window at the stark walls of the White Tower, then brought his eyes slowly back to Dick's face.

"She is my daughter, that's all," he said.

21

His daughter! Hope Joyner the daughter of a master thief! Dick could only look at him, speechless.

"Nobody else knows this but you," Trayne went on, "though I suspect that the old woman Ollorby guesses."

"Your daughter?"

Trayne shrugged his broad shoulders.

"We'll go into that matter another time," he said. "I want you to come with me now to save Hope – and something else. Do you know a good flying officer, a man you can trust?"

"I am a pilot," said Dick quietly. "I think I could get a machine. Do you know where she is?"

The Tiger nodded.

"I want nothing said about this. I'm trying to float a life raft for myself – you don't understand what I mean."

"I think I do," said Dick in a low voice. "You may save yourself, Trayne, but are you going to float my brother into safety?"

Tiger Trayne bit his lip.

"He was recognised, eh? That complicates matters. However, I'm not worrying even about myself. Hope has always come first. Can you leave the Tower?"

Dick thought rapidly.

"I think I can," he said, "but I shall have to see the Colonel. Will you come with me?"

The man did not answer, but followed him down the stairs and across the square towards the Colonel's house. The policeman was waiting at the head of the steps and they were free from all danger of being overheard, yet neither man spoke.

Leaving Trayne outside, Dick went into the house, and the Tiger, his hands in his pockets, marched up and down, for all the world as though he were a civilian sentry posted to guard the premises. Five minutes, ten minutes passed, and then he saw a curtain move and, stopping, looked up. Lady Cynthia was staring down at him, wide-eyed with wonder and fear. She disappeared instantly, and a few seconds later the door of the Colonel's quarters opened and she came out.

"What do you want?" Her voice was harsh; he saw her bosom rise and fall in her agitation.

"Hope Joyner has been carried off by that Eastern swine."

"Hope Joyner?" She repeated the words slowly. "Oh, my God! She isn't – "

"Hope Joyner is my daughter, that's all I can tell you," he said. "I've kept her out of my rotten life, given her the position and the comfort of a lady, looked after her, cared for her from that day I rescued her from the damned baby-farmer to whom her mother had given her. Hope Joyner!" He rasped the words. "Whose family isn't good enough for the Colonel's wife! Remember that, Cynthia."

She put out her hand against the wall of the house to steady herself. She was the colour of chalk; her knees hardly supported her.

"A fellow named Warrington has got her. She's en route to Kishlastan – and I guess I know by what ship. Now don't make a fool of yourself." His voice was rough, but there was kindliness in it, that she at any rate could recognise, and she nodded.

"I'll go into the house," she said faintly, and as she turned to drag her leaden feet from him she looked back. "You'll tell me...what happens?"

"I will let you know," he said, and at that moment Dick came out.

"It is all right!" he said – he hardly noticed Lady Cynthia. "The Colonel has been a brick; fortunately one of the Government people was with him."

"What did you tell them?" asked Trayne, as they hurried down the slope, the policeman quickening his steps to follow them.

"I hinted that you could get the crown back, and they jumped at the chance. The papers haven't the story yet, and they'd give anything in the world to keep the news out of the Press."

In defiance of all speed regulations, Trayne's car rushed them to Kenley, the nearest military aerodrome. The commandant had been advised by telephone of their coming, and a scout machine was waiting.

Five minutes after they had reached the ground the little machine zoomed up into the cloudy skies and headed eastward

22

Graham Hallowell was glad to get back to his cabin, which, compared with the dark, wet deck, was a place of comfort and cheer. He locked the door on himself and went to look for Colley. The man was sitting in a corner of his dark cubby hole, his face in his hands. He looked up as Graham opened the door, his teeth chattering.

"I thought it was that brute," he said tremulously. "Where have they put her?"

"I don't know."

"I was to have had the port cabin. Which is the port side?"

Graham thought it unnecessary to answer so puerile a question. He fastened back the bulkhead door securely.

"You'd better sit in my – stateroom!" he suggested, without any great enthusiasm. "I'm going out again, but I shall lock the door on you, so you needn't be scared."

"What are you going to do?" asked the shivering Colley.

"I don't know. This fellow must put Hope ashore, whatever happens."

He stepped out again into the alleyway, carefully locking the door, and made a search, first of the cabins on that side of the ship, and, when these had produced no sign of Hope Joyner, he went back to the well to investigate the other alleyway which ran the length of the superstructure. But here he was baffled: the alleyway was closed by an iron door, which was fastened on the inside. He climbed the ladder that led to the little boat deck and made an unsteady progress until he was under the shelter of the small navigating bridge. Here he could see two figures standing together in one corner of the bridge, but apparently they had not seen him.

Keeping under the bridge, he crossed the deck to the port side. A ladder led to the fore well, but he saw that if he descended this he must be observed. Wriggling his body, feet first, over the edge of the deck, he dropped to the well below. His manoeuvre was successful. The entrance of the port alleyway had a door, and it was open.

The little ship was now rolling and tossing like a toy boat in a gale of wind. He was buffeted from side to side, but happily he was a good sailor and felt no distress from the motion.

The first cabin he investigated was evidently shared by the two brothers. A foul hole of a place, littered with dirty bedclothes, half-wet oilskins, and two empty bottles that rolled from side to side with every movement of the ship. The next cabin was Eli's own. It was larger, but as unsavoury as the others. The third and last of the cabins was locked. He tried the door gingerly and, stooping, peered through the keyhole. There was no sign of life. To knock would be to alarm her, without serving any useful purpose.

A few steps brought him to the iron door leading into the aft well. It was bolted top and bottom, and these he drew back and, opening the door, stepped out on to the deck, closing the door behind him.

He saw nobody, not even a deck hand. Apparently the "crew" were all employed in the engine-room, the *Pretty Anne* carrying no deck hands at all. Colley, limp and seasick, had crawled back to the dark inner cabin when Graham returned to gather a couple of blankets and a pillow. He turned the lock on his wretched companion, and going back to the port alleyway, he fastened the iron door and, sitting down in a corner, fell into an uneasy sleep.

He did not hear the coming of Eli Boss nor the opening of a door. But the girl who crouched on the bunk came to her feet at the sound of the key in the lock.

"Now let's have a look at you."

He had shut the door behind him – this was the sound that woke Graham – and was lighting a lantern.

Hope Joyner stood by the bunk, both hands gripping its wooden side, her steady eyes surveying the hideous face that peered into hers. Eli Boss had hung the lantern on a hook and was now feasting his eyes on this unexpected vision of loveliness. She saw them open wider and wider in his amazement, till they were round circles of pale blue fire. And even when the big, dirty hand came out towards her face, she did not flinch; did not even scream when it touched her smooth cheek. The ugly bearded mouth was agape.

"A beauty, eh, lass? I've never seen nothing like you – like satin, you are, to the touch."

She shrank back from those caressing paws, and the sight of her fear seemed to madden the man, for of a sudden her shoulders were gripped and she was drawn towards him.

"A beauty…!" he mumbled.

And then something hard pressed in the middle of his back, and he relaxed his hands, turned slowly, and as he turned, the iron thing that prodded him rammed round his waist. He looked down first at the pistol and then into Graham's set face.

"What's the idea?" he said, breathing hard. "Thought you hadn't got a gun?"

In reply, Graham jerked his head towards the door.

"What's the idea?" asked Eli Boss again. The muzzle of the pistol was pressing against his stomach. To drop his hands meant death, as he knew… "Thought you hadn't got a gun, eh?"

"Get outside," said Graham shortly.

The big man hesitated, then went clumping slowly to the door. He was two feet away when he leapt, but Graham had been expecting something of the sort, and he was through the doorway before it could close.

"Boss, I'll shoot you like a dog if you give me any further trouble! I'll shoot you and drop you over the side, and your damned sons will never know what became of you. Colley Warrington is in my cabin – that makes you jump! There's an attempted murder charge hanging over you, my man!"

"What's the idea…?" Eli Boss had a limited vocabulary.

"I'll explain to you later. Go back to the bridge, and leave that key."

Graham snatched the key from the lock and put it in his pocket. Without a word the old man shuffled off into the darkness. In an instant Graham had opened the door and beckoned the girl.

"You will be much safer in my cabin," he said. "I'm Graham Hallowell – you guessed that?"

She nodded.

"You'd better bring a blanket and a pillow. I'll fix you up tomorrow."

She did not resist, but carried the blanket and pillow in her hand, and Graham allowed her to carry these, for he wanted freedom to move against any attack which might come. But nobody opposed them, and in a few minutes they were behind the locked door of Graham's room.

"No, I am not sick," she said. "I'm feeling rather – horrible! I think they must have given me chloroform."

He made her lie down on the bunk, covered her over with a blanket, and though she protested that she was not tired, she had hardly closed her eyes before her breathing became regular and she was asleep.

Graham sat down to consider his problem. In the inner cabin was Colley Warrington, a useless encumbrance. He, too, had fallen into a sleep of exhaustion. He sat on a stool, his elbows on his knees, and tried to arrive at the realities of this grotesque situation. For the greater part of an hour he sat thus, thinking, planning, regretting... then he rose stiffly, unlocked the safe and took out the big case. It was fastened with a spring, which he pressed, and four sides fell apart, and there was revealed a sight so beautiful that it took his breath away. He lifted the crown gingerly, held it in his hand, and then he began to laugh hysterically.

"How funny! How damned funny!" he said.

Presently he steadied himself, replaced the jewel, snapped the covering into place, and pushed it into the safe.

They would give him ten, probably twenty years, but his mind was made up. If he spent the rest of his life in prison, the nose of the *Pretty Anne* would be headed for the shore as soon as daylight came. It should have come by now, he remembered, and with great difficulty unscrewed the deadlights and hinged them up. Yes, dawn had broken. Through the porthole he saw grey tumbling seas and the dark line of land on the horizon, He unscrewed the second deadlight, and this necessitated leaning over the sleeping girl. She woke with a little scream.

"It is all right," he said in a low voice. "I'm getting light and air into this horrible place."

"I'm sorry" – she was almost humble – "I must have been dreaming."

"Go to sleep again," he suggested, but sleep had vanished now.

"Can't we go out? I shall be ill if we don't," she begged.

Graham hesitated.

"Surely," he said, and, unlocking the door, he guided her through the alleyway to the deck.

And here she stood, clasping the bulwarks, and drawing into her lungs the fresh, clean air of the sea. There was nobody about. Graham climbed the ladder cautiously and peeped over. There was no sign of Eli Boss, but a man who he guessed was his son was leaning on the fore rail of the bridge.

In a few words Hope told him how she had come aboard, and he was able to supplement her information.

"To India?" she gasped. "How terrible!" And then, as the solution flashed upon her: "Is it the Prince?… I mean, is he behind this?"

"I guess so," said Graham curtly; "but we're not going to India. As soon as you're back in the cabin I'm interviewing Mr Eli Boss, and his sailing plans will undergo a little change. And then – "

The marlinspike flung by an unsteady, drunken hand missed his head, but struck him on the shoulder, and he turned with a gasp of pain as Eli Boss launched himself over the edge of the upper deck, followed by two of his tatterdemalion crew. The first shot brought the negro seaman to his knees; before he could fire again, Eli had dodged through the narrow door of the port alleyway, out of range. The second of the seamen, squealing at the top of his voice, flew into the starboard passage and slammed the iron door behind him. Graham threw himself against the door, but before he could move he heard a bolt driven home. He was cut off from his cabin, from the jewel!

He tried the other alleyway: that, too, had been closed. The only way left was the ladder to the upper deck. He took two steps, his head had hardly appeared above the deck, before something whizzed past his ear and there was the deafening report of a rifle shot.

And then he heard another sound: somebody was hammering at the door of his cabin. It could be opened on the inside by a spring catch, he remembered, and Colley Warrington was so far gone in misery that he had not even troubled to warn him.

Again came the noise of hammering; then the sound of a deep, hateful voice, and a terrified scream, like the squeal of an animal in mortal pain… Then silence.

The girl's face was twitching.

"What is it?" she breathed. "Something dreadful is happening."

He shook his head.

"The most dreadful thing is your presence on this wretched packet!" he said.

He made the girl sit down under the lee of the ship's side, and once more he attempted a reconnaissance. Taking off his coat, he rolled it into a ball and lifted it cautiously above the edge of the upper deck. Immediately came the crack of a rifle; something struck the coat and a ricochetted bullet droned overhead.

"That's that," he said coolly, as he came back to the deck. "We're trapped unless – "

His eyes were on the hatches that covered the afterhold; for he guessed, by the motion of the ship, that she carried precious little cargo.

The afterdeck, he imagined, held the quarters of the crew, but to reach them he must again come under the fire of the marksmen on the bridge.

"I'm awfully hungry," she said, "and thirsty. Could you get water somewhere?"

Rain had fallen heavily in the night, and a little pool had formed on the sagging tarpaulin that covered the hatch.

"It won't be very palatable, but you'd better try that," he suggested. "Keep close under the cover of the upper deck."

The water was fresh, she told him, and after slaking his own thirst he searched in his pockets in the hope of finding something that would stay the pangs of hunger.

The Channel was alive with craft. A big Hamburg boat passed them within rifleshot, but there was no means by which he could communicate, and though he attempted to send a semaphore message, he knew that he could not be seen against the dark background of the well deck.

Once he heard a splash and looked over the side… Something drifted past, twirling round and round till it disappeared in the white wake of the *Pretty Anne.*

"What did you see?" asked the girl.

"Nothing," said Graham.

Had he been a praying man he might have uttered a few supplications for the soul that had gone out of that soiled and mangled body; for he had looked down into the sightless face of what had once been Colley Warrington.

Eleven came, noon, one o'clock. The smell of cooking food was wafted back to them.

"We'll wait till night, then I can rush the bridge," he said huskily.

She had been looking at him curiously, and he wondered what was in her thoughts. Now she spoke.

"You're rather like Dick, aren't you?"

"Too much like him," he said.

He was on the point of telling her of his last night's adventure, but thought it best that she should learn the truth from one who would not attempt to excuse his action.

How was Dick? he wondered, and had just a little pang of remorse at the trouble he had brought upon his brother. His own state was too desperate, however, to allow him to give much thought to the misfortunes of others.

He was looking at his watch at ten minutes after one, when he heard a sound from the deck above; the sound of something being trundled along the iron plates. Then he saw a big cask up-ended at the head of the steps, and thought at first that it was an attempt being made to block his attack along the upper deck. He had scarcely formed this opinion when the cask tumbled slowly over. He had just time to leap to safety before it came down with a crash on the deck.

Out of the corner of his eye he saw the girl crouching against the bulwarks, and then he felt a red-hot pain in his left arm, and knew that he had been forced from cover. He shot down the first man that leapt from the bridge at him, and then they were on him – half a dozen nondescript men, stabbing and hacking and bludgeoning him. He kicked himself free of the press, and, wounded and battered, shot back. He saw Eli Boss clap his hand to his throat and go down in a groaning heap with a bullet through his neck. But the odds were too many; the men on the bridge were shooting at him; bullets smacked against the iron plating of the deckhouse behind him. Again he felt a terrible, maddening pain in his left arm, and in desperation shot back at the figure on the bridge, saw him stagger and drop to his knees. Then, with a yell, a negro greaser, half mad with rage and fright, grappled with him, and he went down under a gouging, clawing mass of brute men who desired nothing but his life....

The little aeroplane had left the dappled green of Kent behind; beneath was the white line of breakers and a grey blue sea, and ships... scores of ships, some heading up, some down Channel, some with their bows towards the French coast, and none at that height seeming to move. Once they saw a ship which seemed to answer the description of the *Pretty Anne* and swooped down on it, only to find it was a big trawler. Left and right the aeroplane ranged, but there was no sign of the *Pretty Anne* until – "That is she!" roared a voice in Dick's ear, and he saw a speck of a boat, broad of beam, and even from that height seeming to be in difficulties. "The *Pretty Anne!*" roared Trayne, and pointed again.

Dick had only a few seconds to make a decision. To drop in the sea ahead of her would be to invite disaster. He could not expect the *Pretty Anne* or Eli Boss to engage in rescue work. There was only one thing to be done. He looked round for the destroyer that had been ordered out to meet him, but she was not in sight.

"I'm going to crash him," said Dick.

He brought the nose of his machine down.

"Get ready to jump."

He shut off his engines and the aeroplane glided nearer and nearer. Then there was a thundering shock, and the nose of the scout smashed through the smoke stack and came to a stop before the buckled bridge.

Tiger Trayne had already unfastened his belt. The collision had flung him violently on to the iron deck, and for a moment he lay stunned. As he crawled to his feet he saw Dick Hallowell running aft, heard the sharp crack of an automatic, and followed him unsteadily. The first man he recognised was Eli Boss, his grey beard streaked red, his horrible eyes staring madly.

"Where's Miss Joyner?"

Eli pointed down, and, looking over the rail, Tiger Trayne saw the white face of the girl who huddled in a corner of the deck. She had fainted. He leapt down the stairs and lifted the inanimate figure, and, as he smoothed her face, spoke to her in muttered, broken words of endearment.

"I think they've settled Graham."

He looked over his shoulder at Dick Hallowell.

"Settled… Graham? Oh, yes."

"Take her."

Dick's arms slipped round the girl, and Tiger Trayne lurched towards the quiet figure that lay on the deck.

At first sight it would seem that the hours of Graham Hallowell were few. He lay in a pool of blood, so motionless that at first Trayne thought the man was dead. Stooping, he made a brief examination –

there were a few years in Tiger Trayne's life when he had "walked" a great London hospital. He listened to the heart, made a superficial examination of the wounds, and saw that the real danger was the mangled arm. He made a rough tourniquet to arrest the bleeding, and then mounted to the upper deck. The engines of the *Pretty Anne* were stopped; the upper deck was a tangle of wreckage. Smashed boats, crumpled smokestack and crazy bridge testified to the force of the impact. And that they had not been killed in that collision was little short of miraculous.

The men who had attacked Graham had melted away to their stations. Only old Eli and Joe, his son, were visible. They stood near the wrecked navigating bridge, looking down at son and brother, the man who had been stricken by Graham's last despairing shot.

"Where is Warrington?" asked Trayne.

"Dunno," growled the old man. "Where in hell do you think he is? I've never seen him."

Trayne looked round.

"Get your men to lower away that boat." It was the little motor launch that had brought the girl from London Bridge to the ship; it was still swinging outboard on its davits. There was some difficulty in collecting the crew for the purpose, but after a while the boat was lowered and towed round to the well deck. But there was no necessity to make that hazardous voyage. The destroyer was coming up to them; was so close that they heard the clang of her telegraph as her captain rang to stop…

23

It is an axiom that Governments are superior to the common law. Four people waited in different moods for the grinding wheels of justice to move. A very weak and indifferent Graham Hallowell, convalescing at a Surrey cottage, had only one complaint.

"It will be hateful, being hauled off to prison, just as I've learnt something about you, Diana."

She smiled down at him.

"It can't happen, Graham. I feel it can't happen. They have their crown back, and not a word got into the newspapers… I don't think they'll dare. But if they do…"

She did not finish her sentence. She knew that if this new tenderness went out of her life, life itself would have no meaning.

Tiger Trayne, conscious that he was under the surveillance of the police, waited with the calmness of a large knowledge. Every morning when his servant brought in the newspaper he made his inevitable inquiry about the weather. At breakfast he complained as assiduously about the quality of the coffee. And though, as he took his walks abroad, he was well aware that a shadow followed him, the fact did not disturb his equanimity, or in any way injure his temper.

Dick Hallowell was more fretful than any, although a hint had been conveyed to him that the incident might be considered as closed.

Lady Cynthia made an unexpected visit to his quarters one afternoon.

"I saw you dining last night at the Ritz," she said. "That very pretty girl was Hope Joyner, wasn't it?"

"Yes," said Dick shortly.

"When are you going to bring her to see me?"

He looked up at her quickly.

"I didn't know that you wanted to see her really, Lady Cynthia. Do you?"

She nodded.

"I always like to see brides before they come into the regiment – and she's coming, Dick, isn't she?"

Dick shook his head.

"I am leaving the regiment, Lady Cynthia."

"You are doing nothing of the kind," she replied, in her old masterful way. "I'd love her to be in the regiment. I want to be a – a mother to her, Dick."

There was something in her tone which made him marvel.

EDGAR WALLACE

BIG FOOT

Footprints and a dead woman bring together Superintendent Minton and the amateur sleuth Mr Cardew. Who is the man in the shrubbery? Who is the singer of the haunting Moorish tune? Why is Hannah Shaw so determined to go to Pawsy, 'a dog lonely place' she had previously detested? Death lurks in the dark and someone must solve the mystery before BIG FOOT strikes again, in a yet more fiendish manner.

BONES IN LONDON

The new Managing Director of Schemes Ltd has an elegant London office and a theatrically dressed assistant – however, Bones, as he is better known, is bored. Luckily there is a slump in the shipping market and it is not long before Joe and Fred Pole pay Bones a visit. They are totally unprepared for Bones' unnerving style of doing business, unprepared for his unique style of innocent and endearing mischief.

EDGAR WALLACE

BONES OF THE RIVER

'Taking the little paper from the pigeon's leg, Hamilton saw it was from Sanders and marked URGENT. *Send Bones instantly to Lujamalababa... Arrest and bring to headquarters the witch doctor.*'

It is a time when the world's most powerful nations are vying for colonial honour, a time of trading steamers and tribal chiefs. In the mysterious African territories administered by Commissioner Sanders, Bones persistently manages to create his own unique style of innocent and endearing mischief.

THE DAFFODIL MYSTERY

When Mr Thomas Lyne, poet, poseur and owner of Lyne's Emporium insults a cashier, Odette Rider, she resigns. Having summoned detective Jack Tarling to investigate another employee, Mr Milburgh, Lyne now changes his plans. Tarling and his Chinese companion refuse to become involved. They pay a visit to Odette's flat and in the hall Tarling meets Sam, convicted felon and protégé of Lyne. Next morning Tarling discovers a body. The hands are crossed on the breast, adorned with a handful of daffodils.

Edgar Wallace

The Joker
(USA: The Colossus)

While the millionaire Stratford Harlow is in Princetown, not only does he meet with his lawyer Mr Ellenbury but he gets his first glimpse of the beautiful Aileen Rivers, niece of the actor and convicted felon Arthur Ingle. When Aileen is involved in a car accident on the Thames Embankment, the driver is James Carlton of Scotland Yard. Later that evening Carlton gets a call. It is Aileen. She needs help.

The Square Emerald
(USA: The Girl From Scotland Yard)

'Suicide on the left,' says Chief Inspector Coldwell pleasantly, as he and Leslie Maughan stride along the Thames Embankment during a brutally cold night. A gaunt figure is sprawled across the parapet. But Coldwell soon discovers that Peter Dawlish, fresh out of prison for forgery, is not considering suicide but murder. Coldwell suspects Druze as the intended victim. Maughan disagrees. If Druze dies, she says, 'It will be because he does not love children!'

1242036R0

Printed in Great Britain by
Amazon.co.uk, Ltd.,
Marston Gate.